'Oh, there is just one thing—please drop the Dr Ryan and call me Alex.'

There was a faint trace of amusement in the brown eyes, and Frances felt her cheeks grow hot. She merely nodded in reply, but when he made no attempt to go, she frowned questioningly. 'Was there anything else?' she faltered at last.

'I was rather hoping that you were going to ask me to call you Frances. "Dr Marriott" is going to be very formal for a whole year.'

'Oh. . .oh, yes.' She was suddenly confused, all the more so by his amusement, which was now only too apparent. 'Yes. . .' she took a deep breath '. . . please call me Frances.'

With a brief nod he was gone, leaving her to sink down into the chair behind the desk, hating herself for the way she seemed to be reacting to him. There was something about him that made her act like a gauche schoolgirl, instead of a qualified doctor.

Laura MacDonald is the pseudonym of the author, who lives in the Isle of Wight. She is married and has a grown-up family. She has enjoyed writing fiction since she was a child, but for several years she has worked for members of the medical profession both in pharmacy and in general practice. Her daughter is a nurse and has also helped with research for Medical Romances.

Previous Title

ISLAND PARTNER

AN UNEXPECTED AFFAIR

BY

LAURA MacDONALD

MILLS & BOON LIMITED
ETON HOUSE   18–24 PARADISE ROAD
RICHMOND   SURREY   TW9 1SR

*First published in Great Britain 1991
by Mills & Boon Limited*

© Laura MacDonald 1991

*Australian copyright 1991
Philippine copyright 1991
This edition 1991*

ISBN 0 263 77179 2

*Set in 10½ on 12 pt Linotron Times
03-9103-48220
Typeset in Great Britain by Centracet, Cambridge
Made and printed in Great Britain*

CHAPTER ONE

As FRANCES MARRIOTT drove on to the promenade she found herself wondering if she'd made a mistake in her choice of town, for there could be few things more depressing than a wet afternoon in a seaside resort. Groups of holiday-makers in brightly coloured plastic anoraks huddled together in shop doorways or sought shelter in cars parked on either side of the road.

The rain lashed against her windscreen and seemed to bounce up from the road ahead. The inside of the car had become heavily steamed up, and with a yellow duster Frances wiped the windscreen and peered up at the Regency-style houses that lined the promenade.

Most of them had been converted into hotels or guest-houses, but she could see nothing she recognised; then just when she was thinking she would have to stop to ask for directions she saw the turning she was looking for. With a thankful sigh she drove into the small cul-de-sac and on to the forecourt of a large, elegant detached house.

There were several cars parked, and Frances quickly pulled into an empty space. Switching off the ignition, she sat for a moment, the rain drumming on the roof, and looked up at the large three-storey building. It was painted white with black wrought-iron balconies at the upstairs windows. A short flight of steps led to the front door, which was flanked by a ramp and two fluted pillars. To the left of the door several brass plates were fixed to the wall.

Frances had only been here once before, and that had been when she'd come for her interview. Now she had arrived to take up the post she had been offered. With another rueful glance at the rain, which gave no indication of easing, she opened the door, picked up her jacket from the back seat and holding it over her head made a dash for the house.

The entrance opened into a wide hallway that led directly on to a large reception and waiting area. Frances removed her jacket and shook it, then closed the door behind her.

A quick glance revealed several patients sitting in the waiting area, which was bright with plants, posters, magazines and an aquarium of brightly coloured tropical fish. Behind the large central desk a young girl was in conversation on the telephone and was simultaneously writing in an appointment book.

Frances paused for a moment to collect herself before approaching the desk. Carefully she smoothed her short dark hair, then adjusted the collar of the crisp white blouse she'd chosen to wear with her grey suit. When she was satisfied she slipped on her jacket.

By this time the girl had replaced the receiver and was looking enquiringly at Frances. She was a bright-faced girl with curly hair and couldn't have been more than eighteen.

'Can I help you?' There was no spark of recognition in her eyes, and Frances realised she was not one of the staff who had been present when she'd previously been shown over the premises.

'Hello, my name is Frances Marriott.' She walked towards the desk, straightening her shoulders as she did so. Of slim build and at five feet nine, Frances was considered tall for a woman and she was conscious that at times she tried to disguise her height. 'Are any of the doctors about?'

The girl looked doubtful. 'Did you want to make an appointment?'

'Oh, no.'

Frances smiled, but before she had a chance to say more the girl continued, 'Well, if you're on holiday, we hold a surgery every morning at eleven o'clock for temporary residents.'

'No, I'm not on holiday. Perhaps I'd better explain.'

The girl had begun to look suspicious, but before either of them had a chance to say anything further one of the doors off the reception area opened and a woman appeared. She looked as if she was in her late fifties, her straight grey hair was cut short and she was dressed in a twin-set and tweed skirt. She glanced at the pair at the desk, looked away, then immediately looked back again.

'Frances!' With her hand outstretched she strode across the floor. 'You've got here—well done! Nice to have you aboard.'

'Dr Lloyd, nice to see you again.' Frances held

out her hand which was immediately grasped in a strong, masculine-like grip.

'The name's Beatrice,' the older woman replied gruffly, then turning to the receptionist she said, 'This is Dr Marriott, Beverley, she's come to join us for a year as Dr Ryan's trainee GP.'

A blush covered the girl's cheeks as Frances smiled at her. 'I'm sorry,' she muttered. 'I didn't know.'

'Beverley's new.' Beatrice Lloyd gave a short laugh that sounded like a bark. 'Have you got your luggage?'

'Yes, it's outside in the boot of the car.' Frances glanced towards the door. 'But it's pouring with rain.'

'Well, in that case, I'll take you up to the staff-room, we'll have a cup of tea, then you can get yourself sorted out.'

Dr Lloyd's attitude invited no resistance, and dutifully Frances followed the stocky little figure up a flight of stairs.

At her interview it had been agreed that a tiny flat at the very top of the building went with the job, and while Frances was apprehensive about living 'over the shop' she was also grateful that she didn't have to start looking for suitable accommodation. She had already decided, however, that if it proved to be too inconvenient she would find somewhere else in due course.

Two other receptionists were in the staff-room finishing their afternoon tea. They greeted Frances cheerfully, and although she remembered both from her interview their names eluded her.

As they disappeared down the stairs and Beatrice brewed more tea Frances gave a rueful grin. 'I'll have to write names down until I get to know everyone.'

'There are rather a lot of us,' Beatrice agreed, 'but don't worry, you'll soon get to know everyone. You won't be seeing Neville Chandler today however—it's his day off—and June, our practice manager, is off sick.' Then, abruptly changing the subject, she asked, 'What hospital is it you've come from?'

'Middleton General.'

'Ah, yes, I remember now.' She poured the tea and handed Frances a cup, indicating for her to take a seat.

The room was comfortable, tastefully decorated and overlooking the sea. Books lined most of the wall space, the rest being taken up by a large noticeboard and one or two good Renoir prints.

'Well, you'll find general practice very different, believe me.' Beatrice sat down, crossing her legs, and Frances noticed that in spite of the time of the year she wore thick lisle stockings and brogue shoes. She wondered if that indicated that the weather was always rough in Pebblecoombe.

'Life can get pretty hectic here,' Beatrice continued, 'especially at this time of the year, but try and take things in your stride and don't let it get to you.'

Frances smiled at the older woman. Already she

had decided she liked Dr Beatrice Lloyd. Maybe she was blunt, but at least you'd know where you stood with her. 'Is it the patients I mustn't let get to me?' Frances raised her eyebrows. 'Or the doctors?'

Beatrice gave her bark again and set down her cup and saucer. 'Both!' she rapped, then stood up, and Frances saw to her surprise that she had swallowed her tea in one go.

'Well, I mustn't dally here.' Beatrice glanced at the man's wrist-watch she wore. 'I've got an antenatal clinic in three minutes. Alex is out on his calls at the moment, but he should be back soon. No, don't get up—finish your tea, then sort yourself out. You can find the way up to your flat, can't you?' Not waiting for Frances to reply, she strode from the staff-room with a wave of her hand.

With a sigh Frances leaned back in the comfortable armchair. She'd already met Dr Alex Ryan, who was to be her trainer, once when he'd come to the hospital for a meeting with herself and her tutors and again when she'd come to the interview at the surgery. She knew little about him except that he was in his early forties, had two children and would become senior partner in the practice when Dr Neville Chandler retired in two years' time. On first acquaintance Frances had found him rather brusque and was left with the distinct impression that he wasn't a man to suffer fools gladly. Consequently she found herself anticipating her traineeship with a certain amount of apprehension.

Standing up, she crossed the room to the high arched windows and spent a few moments staring out at the view. The room was at the back of the house and looked out directly over the bay, the beach and the red cliffs in the distance. She glanced down and saw that below, beyond a small walled garden, there appeared to be a jetty where a rowing-boat was moored. Frances had been pleased when she'd been invited to join this particular practice, for she had always enjoyed being near the sea and swimming was one of her favourite pastimes. Not that there seemed to be much swimming going on today, she thought grimly.

The sea appeared rough, the waves greenish grey in colour and capped with white foam, and as Frances leaned forward across the window-sill she could see a red flag flying from a nearby breakwater. She knew enough from her own childhood holidays by the sea that it was a danger warning to bathers in rough weather. It did, however, appear to have stopped raining, and Frances thought it might be a good opportunity to get her luggage from the car and take it upstairs to her flat.

There seemed to be more activity in the reception area by this time, with patients coming and going, the receptionists busy behind the desk and the phones constantly ringing.

Frances hesitated for a moment, then, before she had a chance to say anything to the girls behind the desk, the front door was suddenly flung open and everyone looked up. A man was standing in the open doorway. He was of medium height and lean build and his short dark hair was just touched with grey.

Frances immediately recognised him. It was Dr Alex Ryan, her trainer. Angrily he looked round at the waiting patients, then at the girls behind the desk. 'I can't get my car in. There's someone in my space,' he snapped.

'Who's parked in Dr Ryan's space, please?' asked one of the receptionists in a loud voice, and Frances got the impression that she'd had to ask the same question many times in the past.

The patients looked at each other and some shook their heads.

'Well, it must belong to someone.' The irate doctor gave a loud sigh. 'And I can't start surgery until I get in.' He stepped back, glancing round the door. 'It's a blue Metro, registration RRN——'

'Oh!' gasped Frances. 'That's mine. I'm sorry, I didn't know that was anyone's particular space.'

He stared at her in exasperation, his hands on his hips, and amid smirks from the patients she hurried to the door. She could feel the colour in her cheeks as she fumbled in her bag for her keys, only too aware that he watched her every move.

'It does say the car park is for doctors. . .' he began, then he frowned. 'Good lord, it's you, Dr Marriott! I didn't recognise you. It's your hair—it's different.' He followed her to her car, and as Frances glanced up she found herself gazing into a pair of most attractive brown eyes.

'Yes, it's me,' she replied quietly as she slipped into her car and started the engine.

With a backward glance she reversed rapidly and drove out of the car park, but not before she'd had the satisfaction of seeing his slightly embarrassed expression.

Outside in the road Frances stopped in front of a dark grey Audi, wondering where on earth she was to park, especially as she had two heavy suitcases to unload. A moment later someone rapped on her window. She wound it down and found herself looking into the same pair of brown eyes.

'Why in heaven's name didn't you say who you were when I was sounding off in Reception?' He sounded irritable now, as if it was still all her fault, and his attitude only increased her fears as to what she could expect in the coming year.

'You didn't give me a chance,' she retorted, then bit her lip. This really wasn't the best of starts to her relationship with her trainer.

Dr Ryan, however, chose not to reply; instead he turned and pointed to a path at the side of the house. 'As you're staying in the flat we thought you could park down there. We really are pushed for space at the front.'

'OK.' Frances put her car into gear.

'You'd do better to reverse in,' he instructed firmly.

She gritted her teeth. 'Very well. Whatever you say.' Almost savagely she drew forward, then as she turned to reverse she realised he was directing her back into the fairly narrow space. It took all her concentration not to touch the gateposts, but she was determined she wouldn't give him the satisfaction of thinking her incompetent. By the time she'd finished the manoeuvre and backed a short distance down the pathway she looked up and saw to her relief that he'd disappeared.

Then she dismissed him from her mind, having far more important issues to contend with. Struggling out of the car in the confined space, she squeezed round the back, opened the boot and yanked out her suitcases.

Awkwardly she tottered back into the road and saw that the grey Audi had gone, then as she turned into the forecourt again she noticed that it was parked where she had been. With a sigh of relief she saw it was empty and guessed that the impatient Dr Ryan had gone to start his surgery. It was as she was struggling up the steps towards the front door that she heard a shout.

'Hi, Frances! Here, let me give you a hand with those.'

Half turning, she found a young suntanned man with a shock of brown hair, and immediately she recognised Simon Mitchell, the fourth and junior partner in the practice.

'Hello, Simon,' she gasped. By this time her arms were weakening with the weight of the cases. 'Nice to see a friendly face!'

Taking the cases from her, he grinned. 'Why? Have they all been unfriendly up until now?'

'No, but let's just say I had a rather unfortunate encounter with Dr Ryan.'

'Alex?' Simon gave a hoot of laughter. 'Oh, don't let him bother you. His bark's worse than his bite.'

'You could have fooled me.' Frances followed him into Reception.

'Do you want these taken up to your flat?' he asked, then when she nodded he gave a mock groan and rolled his eyes. She followed him up the stairs, remembering how after her interview she'd stayed and had coffee and chatted to him, immediately drawn to his warm friendly manner.

On the first floor he paused, set the cases down and flexed his fingers. 'What in the world have you got in these?' He pulled a face. 'The kitchen sink?'

'Practically,' Frances replied with a laugh. 'Here, let me take one of them now.'

'No, I'll soldier on.' With a deep sigh he resolutely picked them up again and plodded up another flight of stairs to the top floor, while Frances followed, thinking how nice it would be working with him.

The flat was tucked away at the back of the house, and like the staff-room on the floor below it boasted sea views from both the sitting-room and the bedroom. It was furnished, and although it was basic Frances knew that she would be able to provide those vital touches that would make it home. Someone had thoughtfully placed flowers in a vase on the coffee-table in the bay window of the sitting-room, a gesture that moved her. Simon set her cases down in the centre of the sitting-room floor and glanced around. 'Are you sure you're going to be all right up here?' he asked doubtfully.

'For the time being, yes,' Frances replied as she peered into the kitchen. 'I may in time look round for something else, but this will be fine for now.'

'Well, if you do want anywhere else, let me know,' he replied with a touch of eagerness. 'I may just be able to fix something up for you. Anyway, it'll be great having you here, it's about time we had some more young blood about the place.' He grinned, then added, 'Mind you, they are rather chucking you in at the deep end, aren't they?'

'What do you mean?' She looked startled. Was there something she hadn't been told?

'Well, they've picked just about the busiest time of year for you to start, with all the TRs here.'

'TRs?' She frowned.

'Temporary residents. Here in their thousands at the moment.'

'Oh, yes, of course. How silly of me! They must increase the workload enormously.' She smiled, then went on to tell him how Beverley had mistaken her for a holiday-maker.

'A natural enough mistake for our Bev, she's only been here a week.' He paused. 'But what was it that Alex did to upset you?'

'I think it was more the other way round. I upset him.'

He grinned at her. 'No, don't tell me. Let me guess. You parked in his car space?'

She stared at him in astonishment. 'How did you guess?'

'Not difficult. It happens all the time, and it's the one thing guaranteed to infuriate Alex.'

'What's he like?' Frances asked, suddenly curious about the man who was to be her trainer for the next year.

'Alex?' Simon hesitated, screwing up his eyes as he considered. 'Oh, he's not a bad sort really. A bit self-opinionated and he occasionally gets uptight over his kids, but apart from that he's OK.'

'How old are his children?'

'Oh, both in their teens—you know, the difficult age. Well, I must get on. I dare say there's a waiting-room full down there for me. What are you going to do about food? Would you like to join me later for dinner?' He looked hopeful.

'I don't think so, Simon, thanks all the same. I'll pop out to the supermarket later, get a few bits and pieces and spend the evening getting myself sorted out.'

'OK,' he replied amiably. 'Perhaps another time, but if there's anything you want just give us a shout. See you later.'

She saw him to the door, thanked him for his help and watched as he clattered down the stairs, then with a little sigh she closed the door and for a moment leaned against it.

Simon Mitchell really did seem very nice, but Frances had a feeling she was going to have to watch the situation where he was concerned. When he had offered to look out for another flat for her she had recognised the look in his eyes. Hadn't she seen the same look so many times before during her relation-ship with Andrew Grant?

She felt a pang as she thought of Andrew. They went back a long way together, having started medi-cal school on the same day. In fact, Frances often thought they had actually grown up together, but where in the first innocence of their affair they had believed their love would last forever, the onset of maturity had decreed otherwise. In the end it had been she who had ended the relationship, albeit reluctantly, but they had both recognised that it had played itself out and they had parted friends.

Now, however, she wanted no emotional involvements, having vowed to herself that her career must, in future, come first.

With a little sigh she glanced round the flat, trying to visualise how she would arrange things when the rest of her gear arrived. It just wouldn't be home until her collection of cats was in position. Frances adored cats; cats of every breed, shape and colour, and over the years she'd built up an extensive collection of feline ornaments that went everywhere with her. It was, to her, the next best thing to having a cat of her own, something that was impossible with her lifestyle. She'd packed the precious collection herself with the rest of her gear in the trunk which was to be delivered the following day.

The next hour Frances spent unpacking her cases and hanging her clothes in the wardrobe, then an investigation in the kitchen showed her that her proposed trip to the shops was quite unnecessary. Someone, probably the same person who had arranged the flowers, had stocked both the store cupboard and the fridge with everything she would need for several days at least.

She was about to start preparing herself a light snack when there came a knock on her door. Thinking it was Simon come back to try to persuade her to change her mind about going out to dinner, she hurried across the sitting-room and pulled open the door.

The smile, however, froze on her face. 'Oh!' she said. 'It's you.'

'I'm sorry to disappoint you.' His reply was cool but the brown eyes were watchful. 'You were obviously expecting someone else. May I come in?'

'Yes, of course.' Slightly flustered, she stepped aside and allowed Alex Ryan into her flat.

CHAPTER TWO

BY THE time Frances had closed the door Alex had walked across to the window and was staring out at the grey scene beyond. He didn't speak immediately, and more to break the silence than anything else Frances found herself saying, 'I hope the weather isn't always like this—I was looking forward to some swimming.'

He turned abruptly and she found him staring at her again in the same way that he had in the car park. 'The forecast is better for tomorrow,' he replied vaguely, glancing around the sitting-room as he spoke. 'Do you have everything you need?' He frowned, drawing his dark brows together.

'For the moment, yes. Some kind person has stocked me up with provisions.' She didn't mention the flowers, instinct telling her they wouldn't have come from him.

'Good. That would have been June, our practice manager—she's a friendly sort. Now, are you sure you're going to be all right up here on your own?'

Frances narrowed her eyes. 'You'll have me feeling nervous in a minute! Simon Mitchell asked me the same question.'

'Simon?' He glanced round suspiciously as if he expected Simon to suddenly appear from the kitchen or the bedroom.

'Yes,' she replied coolly. 'Simon carried my cases up for me.' For the second time that day she had the satisfaction of seeing him look uncomfortable.

'Oh, I see. Well, I'm sure there's no need for you to feel nervous, but I have taken the liberty of arranging a few precautions.' He walked across to the sideboard. 'You have the telephone, of course.' He lifted the receiver to satisfy himself it was working properly. 'And over here I've had a panic button installed in conjunction with our security system. If you press it in an emergency, it will ring in the local police station and you'll have a squad car here within minutes. We know because Doris, our cleaner, accidentally did just that, and had the life frightened out of her when the police arrived.'

'I wouldn't have thought the crime rate was very high in a place like this,' said Frances slowly.

'It isn't particularly,' he replied. 'But a surgery is always an obvious target for drug addicts, and seaside towns do seem to attract more than their fair share of those during the season.'

'Do you keep many drugs on the premises?'

'No, but they don't know that. Besides, it isn't only drugs they're after, it's blank prescription pads and empty syringes. Still, I don't want you worrying about it because I'm sure we've taken adequate steps to prevent any trouble.'

'When would you like me to start work?'

He gave her a sharp glance. 'I thought the sixteenth was the date we agreed. That's tomorrow, isn't it?'

She nodded. 'It is, and I'm quite prepared to start

tomorrow. What I really meant was, where do I
start?'

He seemed to relax a little as he considered, but
Frances thought she still detected a trace of hostility
in his attitude towards her. Maybe it was because of
the earlier incident over the parking, but she
wouldn't have thought he would have let such a
trivial thing affect his judgement of her. Whatever it
was, she hoped he got over it quickly. A year was a
long time, and if she was to gain the experience she
needed she wanted at least a pleasant working
relationship with her trainer.

'I think it will be best tomorrow if you spend the
morning getting familiar with the building and the
rest of the staff and arranging your consulting-room.'
He paused, reflecting for a moment, and it crossed
Frances's mind again what an attractive-looking man
he was, with his dark colouring, the flecks of grey in
his hair and his classic profile.

'We'll meet up after lunch,' he continued, quite
unaware of her scrutiny and assessment of his looks,
'discuss your schedule, then you can sit in on afternoon surgery with me. Will that suit you for your
first day?'

He raised his eyebrows as he waited for her reply,
and she coloured slightly as she thought she detected
a touch of patronage in his tone.

'Of course,' she replied briskly, then, determined
not to let him think she was in any way intimidated
by him, she added, 'Now, if you'll excuse me, please,
I have things to do.'

He looked a little surprised at her obvious dismissal but he made no comment and walked to the door, where he paused, one hand on the Yale catch, and turned and stared at her yet again.

'What is it?' she was finally forced to ask. 'Is there something wrong?'

'It's your hair. . .'

'My hair?' Frances put a hand to the shiny dark hair that framed her face. 'What's the matter with it?' It was the second time he'd mentioned her hair, and she couldn't imagine why.

'There's nothing the matter with it. It's just that you look so different. I didn't recognise you earlier, you looked completely different from how I remembered you from the interview.'

She gave a faint smile. 'Yes, I have changed the style. At the hospital I always wore it long and in a bun and I didn't have a fringe in those days. I decided it was time for a different image to go with my new lifestyle, but I hadn't realised it was quite so drastic.' She gave a little laugh, but he didn't comment further, merely wishing her goodnight and disappearing down the stairs.

Frances closed the door, dropped the catch and secured the safety chain, puzzling as she did so over whether he had meant to imply that her new image was an improvement or a disaster. She finally came to the conclusion that she simply didn't know. Like so many doctors, Alex Ryan seemed to be the type of man who gave away very little about his feelings.

By the time Frances got to bed that night she'd forgotten any slight misgivings she might have had about being alone at the top of the building. As her head touched the pillow she briefly heard the patter of rain against the windowpane before she fell into a deep sleep.

She awoke to bright sunlight, the cries of seagulls and, from somewhere in the building, the comforting hum of a vacuum cleaner. For a moment she couldn't remember where she was then, as memory flooded back, she gave a sigh and turned over. Today was her first day in general practice. She lay for a few minutes collecting her thoughts, then she got out of bed, stretched and crossed to the window, throwing back the floral curtains.

A vastly different scene from that of the night before met her eyes, immediately lifting her spirits. In complete contrast to the grey tossed waves of yesterday, the sea was as smooth as glass with barely a ripple to disturb its surface. One or two yachts were at anchor in the bay, the points of their masts glistening in the early morning sunlight, while overhead black-headed gulls circled and swooped in their quest for food.

This was more like it, thought Frances happily. This was the sort of thing she'd been hoping for when she'd been told she would be going to Pebblecoombe. Humming softly to herself, she showered and dressed and made some tea, then before making toast for her breakfast she decided a little fresh air wouldn't come amiss and that she would go in search of a morning paper.

She ran lightly down the stairs and on the first

floor found Doris the cleaner going about her morning chores. When she saw Frances she switched off her vacuum.

'Hello, love.' She had an honest friendly face and large capable hands that looked as if they'd seen a lifetime of hard work. 'You must be Dr Marriott. I was told you'd be here—Dr Ryan left me a message so's I wouldn't think we had burglars. Did you sleep all right?'

'Yes, thank you, Doris—like a top. Can you tell me where I can get a newspaper?'

'Yes, love. Go out of here and turn left. About a hundred yards down the road opposite the pier, there's a tobacconist. He sells papers as well.'

On the ground floor everything appeared strangely quiet and empty. Even the piles of magazines in the waiting area were neat and tidy and each of the consulting-room doors stood open to air the rooms before the morning onslaught.

Frances let herself out, carefully locking the door behind her. At the top of the steps she paused and looked around, taking in great lungfuls of the fresh, almost heady sea air. Suddenly she had a feeling that everything was going to be all right. Maybe she had even imagined the slightly hostile attitude of her trainer, she thought hopefully as she set off walking briskly out of the cul-de-sac on to the promenade.

There were few people about, mostly tradesmen or early morning tourists who, like herself, had come out for newspapers or to take advantage of the beautiful morning. As she left the shop she crossed the road and paused for a moment by the railing, admiring the sea view.

One or two longshoremen were preparing their sites for the day, stacking piles of deckchairs on to tractor-driven trailers to be deposited further along the beach.

A lone swimmer was several yards offshore, cleaving the water with strong clean strokes that caused hardly a ripple. Frances watched enviously, wondering if she would have a moment later in the day to take a dip herself. Maybe in the evening there would be time, after surgery. At the thought of surgery her heart gave an uncomfortable lurch and she knew that, in spite of her earlier optimistic frame of mind, she was dreading her first surgery with Dr Ryan. She had the feeling that her nervousness would show and he would end up thinking her incompetent.

With a sigh she made as if to turn from the rail just as the swimmer left the sea and began to walk up the beach. With a jolt Frances realised that it was Alex Ryan.

She was just wondering if she should walk away when he waved and she knew he had seen her. She stood with one hand on the rail and watched as he walked towards her. He wore the briefest of black swimming-trunks and tiny droplets of water glistened on his lean bronzed limbs and the triangle of black hair on his chest. She suddenly felt embarrassed, as if she'd been caught spying.

He nodded to her and grabbed a towel that was draped over an upturned rowing-boat. 'I see you're an early riser as well,' he said as he vigorously rubbed himself dry.

'Yes.' She glanced at her watch and saw that it still wasn't even seven o'clock. 'Do you swim every morning?'

'Whenever I can.' He looked up her and smiled, and with a start Frances realised it was the first time she had seen him smile. It transformed his face, relieving it of tension and making him look much younger. 'Do you like swimming?' he asked.

'She nodded. 'Yes, very much.'

While they'd been talking he'd pulled on a towelling beach robe, and she was just wondering if he intended walking back to the surgery like that, when he pointed along the beach. 'I go in the back way,' he said. 'See you later.'

With a wave of his hand he was gone, jogging along the beach. As Frances strolled back to the surgery at a more leisurely pace she remembered the jetty that she'd seen at the back of the house, the moored rowing-boat and the tiny walled garden, and she decided there could be more advantages to her new job than she had at first realised.

Much to her surprise Simon's MG was parked in the car park, and as she passed it she wondered if the entire practice were early risers or merely just workaholics.

She found Simon in Reception talking to someone on the telephone while Doris was handing him a steaming mug of coffee.

With a sympathetic look Doris shook her head 'Poor lad,' she muttered. 'Been up half the night, he has.' With that she picked up a duster and a tin of polish and returned to her work.

Frances had intended going straight up to her flat, but decided instead to wait until Simon had finished on the phone and have a word with him.

At last, with a sigh, he replaced the receiver and glanced up at her. 'Good morning.' He nodded, and immediately Frances could see that he looked shattered.

'Bad night?' She knew how he felt, having suffered in the same way during her many night duties as a houseman.

'Yes, seven calls.' He yawned, passing a hand over his mouth and the dark stubble on his chin.

'Any of my patients?' The sudden voice behind them made them both turn. Alex Ryan had come in so quietly from the back of the house that neither of them had heard him. Frances saw that he had discarded the beach robe and was dressed in grey trousers and an open-necked striped shirt.

'Hello, Alex,' Simon replied wearily. 'Let's see now—yes, one of them was yours. Mrs Brown. She had another CVA at about midnight. I admitted her.' When Alex nodded, he went on, 'Oh, and that last call was one of yours.' As he spoke he handed him a set of notes, and as Alex read the name on the front he added, 'Severe pain in her left side and lower back for best part of the night. Husband is very concerned and wants a visit. I'll just drink this coffee, then I'll get over there.'

'No, it's all right, Simon. I'll go,' replied Alex, and when Simon would have protested he added,

'You get yourself shaved and sorted out before surgery.'

The junior partner needed no second bidding, and with a mumbled 'thanks' he ambled off up the stairs to the rest-room, yawning profusely as he went.

As Frances was about to follow him, Dr Ryan intervened. 'How do you fancy doing an early morning house call?'

She paused, one hand on the banister, and swallowed. 'Do you mean on my own?' She turned hesitantly.

'Of course not. I mean you to come with me.'

'Oh. . . Oh, I see. Well, yes, of course.'

'Right, I'll just get my case.' He strode off to his consulting-room, returning seconds later to stare at Frances, who still stood at the foot of the stairs as if transfixed. 'Wouldn't it be an idea if you were to get your case, Dr Marriott?' He said it with a touch of exasperated humour, but it was enough to galvanise Frances into action, and she ran up the stairs without a backward glance, only too aware that he was standing in Reception watching her.

In her flat she only had time to grab her case and her jacket. Ruefully she reflected that she'd had no breakfast, then decided that was the least of her problems. She had almost prepared herself for her first surgery with Dr Ryan, but she hadn't expected her first consultation to be a house call, and certainly not so early in the morning.

A quick glance in the mirror showed that she looked reasonably presentable, although she'd not had the time to apply her usual light make-up.

When she joined Dr Ryan again in Reception she found he was now wearing a dark-coloured jacket and was fastening his tie.

'Right, if you're ready, we'll go.' He barely gave her a glance as they hurried outside. 'We'll take my car,' he said, much to her relief. She'd had a feeling he was going to expect her to drive him to the patient's house. She knew she was going to have to get familiar with the area, but just for the moment she felt she had more than enough to contend with.

The patient, young and newly married, lived in a terrace house on the far side of the town. It took them about fifteen minutes to get there through the steadily mounting morning traffic.

Apart from giving Frances a brief history of the patient they were about to see, Dr Ryan remained silent, a fact for which Frances was grateful as it gave her a chance to collect her thoughts.

As they drew up outside the house, however, he said, 'I'd like you to examine the patient. Tell me your diagnosis and what treatment you intend giving. Is that clear?'

She nodded, but as they got out of the car her heart was pounding.

The patient's husband met them at the dor. He'd obviously been on the look-out and was extremely worried. He frowned suspiciously at Frances but, when Dr Ryan introduced her and he realised she was another doctor, he seemed to accept the fact and showed them both upstairs to the bedroom.

Dr Ryan went in first and greeted his patient who,

although obviously in a lot of pain, seemed pleased and relieved to see him.

'Now, Susan,' he said calmly, 'I've brought Dr Marriott to see you. She would like to examine you, and I'd like you to tell her what seems to be the problem.'

As Frances moved forward and her eyes met those of the patient, her nervousness seemed to evaporate and she smiled reassuringly. Why should she feel nervous? After all, hadn't she done this many, many times before? The only difference then had been that her patients had been in hospital beds.

'Hello, Susan,' she said quietly as she sat on the edge of the bed. 'Would you like to tell me all about it? When did the pain start?'

'Well, I've had it for a couple of days, here in my side, Doctor. I didn't bother to come to the surgery because I thought it'd go away. But it didn't, it got worse, then in the night it moved round to my back.'

'I see.' Frances lifted back the bedclothes. 'Now if you could just lift your nightie and let me look at your tummy.' Gently but thoroughly she carried out her examination, asked the patient more questions about whether she'd had any vomiting or pain on passing urine and what form of contraception she was using. Some of her questions were answered by the patient and some by her husband, who hovered anxiously in the doorway.

When she had finished she rearranged the covers, then stood up and turned to Dr Ryan.

'My diagnosis is pyelitis, but I would like to do an MSU test to be sure. Can we arrange that now?'

He nodded and opening his case handed her a sterile specimen pot. 'We have a collection at the surgery later in the morning from the path lab, so it can go with those. The result will be back tomorrow,' he added.

'Right; while we're waiting for that I would prescribe a broad-spectrum antibiotic, changing it if necessary when the results are known. I would also prescribe a strong analgesic for the pain, and I'd like to arrange for an IVP,' she said firmly.

'What's that?' The woman looked frightened and turned towards Dr Ryan, who indicated for Frances to explain.

'I believe, Susan,' said Frances firmly, 'that you have inflammation of the kidneys, and an IVP is an X-ray which will be done at the local hospital. But first I would like you to give me a mid-stream sample of your urine.' She handed her the specimen pot. 'Do you think you could do that now for me?'

The woman nodded and cautiously climbed out of bed, then assisted by her husband disappeared to the bathroom.

While she was gone Frances wrote out a prescription for an antibiotic and dihydrocodeine tablets on one of Dr Ryan's pads. When the patient returned and handed her the pot, she labelled it, while Susan climbed painfully back into bed.

'You should get the appointment in a day or two.' Frances stood up and snapped her case shut. 'In the meantime I want you to stay in bed and get started on these tablets as soon as possible.' She handed the prescription to Susan's husband. 'Oh, and one more thing—I would like you to drink as much fluid as you can.'

'What sort of fluids, Doctor?' asked the husband.

'Barley water, preferably,' replied Frances. 'At least three pints a day over and above what you usually drink.'

'Thank you, Doctor.' The girl managed a weak smile, and even her husband had a respectful look on his face for Frances as he showed them out of the bedroom.

They took their leave after promising another visit the following day. On the journey back to the surgery Dr Ryan made no comment on the way Frances had handled the visit, offering neither praise nor criticism, something which she found slightly unnerving.

As he negotiated the traffic, she took the opportunity to study him a little more closely. She had known he was in his early forties and had already in her own mind acknowledged his striking good looks. She knew that if he weren't married, and if she hadn't recently decided that men weren't going to play an important role in her life in the immediate future, she could have found him very attractive.

Even as the thought entered her mind a smile touched her lips. Perhaps it was just as well he was out of reach, for his attitude towards her had been far from encouraging. She stole another surreptitious glance at him and, sure enough, once again his mouth was set in an uncompromising line as he studied the road ahead.

He must have sensed her scrutiny, however, for he suddenly threw her a glance.

'Were you about to say something?' he asked abruptly.

'No,' she replied. 'I was just thinking.'

'What about?' It was almost a demand and took her unawares.

'Oh. . .nothing much, just that I'll have to get to know the neighbourhood,' she lied.

He nodded. 'Yes, the sooner the better. I have a map back at the surgery that you can use.'

He was silent then until they drew on to the surgery forecourt, then he looked at his watch. 'There's at least half an hour before anything starts happening. My guess is you didn't have any breakfast, so we'll see you a bit later.' Getting out of his car, he slammed the door and, without waiting for her, strode off inside.

Frances followed more slowly and finding Reception empty she made her way up to her flat, where she made herself toast and coffee before going downstairs to officially begin her first day in general practice.

CHAPTER THREE

BEATRICE LLOYD was in Reception talking to a pleasant-faced, middle-aged woman, whose fair hair was fashionably cut, accentuating the smartness of her appearance. Frances recognised her as June Ritchie, the practice manager, and as she approached both women they looked up.

'Ah, here she is,' boomed Beatrice. 'Raring to go, are we?'

Frances smiled and June Ritchie held out her hand. 'Hello, Frances—nice to see you again. Sorry I wasn't here to welcome you yesterday.'

'Hello, June.' Frances's hand was clasped in a warm handshake. 'I understand you weren't well. Nothing serious, I hope?'

'Only a paralysing migraine—with me a twenty-four-hour job in a darkened room, I'm afraid. Would you like to come into my office for a few minutes? There are one or two forms I need you to sign.' As she was speaking June turned to Beatrice. 'I'll arrange that appointment you wanted at the orthopaedic clinic, Dr Lloyd.'

'Thank you, June—see you later, Frances.' Beatrice Lloyd disappeared into her consulting-room, leaving Frances to follow the practice manager into her office.

The room was bright, catching the morning sun-light, and apart from the huge pile of unopened mail on the desk it was meticulously tidy with its filing cabinets, word processor and wall charts. The only adornments were a profusion of healthy-looking plants that cascaded from the shelves or filled empty corners.

'Are you really feeling better this morning?' Frances asked as she took a seat while June took off her jacket and put her handbag into a cupboard.

The older woman nodded. 'Yes, thanks; a bit fragile still, but it'll pass as the morning goes on. There isn't time to feel sorry for yourself around here! Now, how about you? Have you settled in all right upstairs?'

Frances smiled. 'Yes, and I believe I have you to thank for making the flat so welcoming. The food saved me a lot of time and effort, and the flowers were a lovely gesture.'

'Flowers?' June frowned. 'I'll take credit for the food, but I must confess I don't know anything about any flowers. You must have a secret admirer.'

Frances looked puzzled. 'Well, I can't think who.'

'Probably Dr Mitchell. It's the sort of thing he'd do.' She laughed. 'Have you seen him yet?'

'Yes, he carried my cases in yesterday, and you're probably right about the flowers. He already asked me out to dinner last night.'

'Did he indeed? My word, he didn't waste any time.' Leaning forward, June switched on her computer and typed in her password, then curiously she added, 'Did you go?'

'No, I didn't.' Frances laughed. 'I had far too much to do and I was tired. Besides, I don't want him getting any ideas.'

'Oh, he will. Believe me, he will. You'll have to watch our Simon.' Taking a file from a drawer, June glanced through some papers and passed two across to Frances for her to sign. 'Have you seen Dr Ryan yet?'

'Oh, yes,' replied Frances, and there must have been something in the tone of her voice that caused June to glance sharply at her.

'Is anything wrong?'

'No, not really.' Frances sighed, then went on to explain about the incident in the car park and the early morning house call. 'I'm not sure what it is.' She threw June an uncertain look, not sure how much she should confide, then, after hesitating for a moment longer, she added, 'He seems rather abrupt towards me.'

'Don't worry about it,' June replied firmly. 'He's been under rather a lot of stress lately, but he really is a very good doctor and, from what I've heard, an excellent trainer. Now,' she added briskly, 'what's your programme for today?'

'Well, Dr Ryan said to get familiar with the building, talk to the rest of the staff and generally get to know everyone. I have to meet him after lunch to discuss my training schedule, then I'm to sit in on one of his surgeries.'

June looked at her keenly. 'You're dreading it, aren't you?'

Frances gave a rueful laugh. 'Not nearly so much as when he'll be sitting in on a surgery of mine!'

They were still laughing when there was a sudden tap at the door and Dr Ryan strode in. He glanced at each of them in turn, and the smile froze on Frances's face.

'Good morning, June,' he said briefly. 'Is Neville in yet?' When June shook her head, he turned to Frances. 'Are you going to follow through your pyelitis diagnosis and do an X-ray form?'

'Oh, yes, of course.' She coloured slightly, wondering if he had expected her to do it automatically.

'If you go out to Reception one of the girls will give you a form. Is my post ready yet, June?'

'Not yet, Dr Ryan,' June replied calmly. 'I'll bring it through as soon as it's sorted.'

'Did you want me for anything else?' Frances asked as she replaced the top on her pen and handed the forms back to June. The older woman shook her head, and Frances stood up. 'In that case, I'll go and get my X-ray request form.' Leaving Dr Ryan in the office, she went out to the desk where Lynne, another of the receptionists, gave her the form she wanted. She began to fill it in, then realised she couldn't complete it without the patient's records, and so far as she knew Dr Ryan still had those. She hesitated, wondering if she dared approach him, when he suddenly appeared beside her. It was obvious he'd had the same thought, for he had the necessary records in his hand.

Glancing at his watch, he said, 'I have a few minutes before surgery—come along to the room we've prepared for you and you can write your form there.'

At that moment there was a sudden commotion at the front entrance and the waiting area was filled with at least a dozen foreign students who all seemed to be talking at the same time. Two of them were supporting one young lad who was hopping on one foot. His ankle looked badly swollen. Dr Ryan raised his eyebrows at Lynne, who seemed to visibly brace herself to deal with the situation.

Frances's consulting-room had once been a store-room, but a little thought had been put into the conversion and she found she was delighted with the result. Admittedly it was small, but, from what she had heard from other trainees, she was extremely lucky to have a room of her own. The usual procedure was for the trainee to use the room of whichever doctor happened to be away, either on holiday or on a day off. This arrangement worked well until the inevitable happened and all partners were working on the same day.

The room had been tastefully decorated with pale green paint and darker green carpet tiles and window blinds. Floral-patterned curtains concealed an examination couch while the desk, positioned in front of the window, boasted the usual office implements plus a computer screen and keyboard.

'Are you familiar with these monsters?' asked Dr Ryan, pointing to the terminal as Frances followed him into the room.

'More or less,' she replied cautiously. 'We had

them at the hospital, although I didn't use them that often.'

'We had the system installed about a year ago. Simon swears by it, says he now couldn't manage without one, while Neville, on the other hand, can't seem to get the hang of them.'

'What about you?' She threw him a glance and saw a frown had creased his forehead.

'I'm not sure. For things like drug reports, cervical smear recalls, and repeat prescribing, I'll admit they save time, but there are other times when something goes wrong and I end up exasperated and thinking it would have been easier to have done the whole thing by hand.'

'I'll have to get someone to explain the system to me,' Frances replied doubtfully.

'I'm sure Simon will be only too happy to oblige,' Dr Ryan observed drily. 'Now, let's get down to more practical matters.' He handed her the records of the patient they'd seen that morning. 'There are the notes for your X-ray request.'

'Thank you.' She placed them on her desk and turned back to him. 'You said yesterday, Dr Ryan, that you wanted me to spend the morning getting familiar with everything. Did you have anything specific in mind?'

He nodded, and she was struck by how decisive he seemed. 'Yes, I want you to spend time with the girls in Reception. Get them to show you how the whole system works—they're a nice bunch of girls, I'm sure you'll get on well with them. It might also be a good idea to talk to Sandra.'

'Sandra?'

'You haven't met her yet?' When Frances shook her head, he continued. 'She's the practice nurse. She works in the treatment room and has her own appointment system.' He paused, hesitating for a moment, then apparently choosing his words carefully he said, 'You may find Sandra can be a bit difficult at times, but she's a good nurse and does her job well. Now, is there anything you want to ask before I go and start my surgery?'

'I don't think so, thank you, Dr Ryan.'

He turned to the door, then paused. 'Oh, there is just one thing—please drop the Dr Ryan and call me Alex.'

There was a faint trace of amusement in the brown eyes, and Frances felt her cheeks grow hot. She merely nodded in reply, but when he made no attempt to go, she frowned questioningly. 'Was there anything else?' she faltered at last.

'I was rather hoping that you were going to ask me to call you Frances. "Dr Marriott" is going to be very formal for a whole year.'

'Oh. . .oh, yes.' She was suddenly confused, all the more so by his amusement, which was now only too apparent. 'Yes. . .' she took a deep breath '. . .please call me Frances.'

With a brief nod he was gone, leaving her to sink down into the chair behind the desk, hating herself for the way she seemed to be reacting to him. There was something about him that made her act like a gauche schoolgirl instead of a qualified doctor.

She glanced round the room, then resolutely she

squared her shoulders and decided that she wouldn't be intimidated by anyone; apprehensive she might be, but she would not be patronised. Briskly she filled in the X-ray request form, then spent the next half-hour arranging the room to her liking. Finally she reached the point where she could do no more until her books arrived, so she made her way back to Reception.

The scene that met her eyes appeared to be one of organised chaos, for, although the whole area was packed with waiting patients, the phones ringing continuously, the doctors' buzzers sounding and a constant stream of people coming and going, the girls behind the desk seemed to be in complete control. With calm efficiency, they directed and organised, giving help or advice where necessary.

June was in the office area behind the desk which housed the practice filing system, and when she saw Frances she beckoned to her, then proceeded to show her around.

Carefully she explained everything; how new patients registered with a doctor, the method they used for repeat prescribing, the appointment and house call system, and even how the intercom worked on the telephone.

The girls were friendly and cheerful and seemed only too willing to help Frances and explain their various jobs. Just when she thought her head would burst with so many facts, June said, 'Now, I think it's time you met Sandra.' She looked at Lynne. 'Is she very busy at the moment?'

Lynne glanced at an appointment book on the

desk. 'She's removing stitches,' she replied, then looked up quickly as a door opposite the desk suddenly opened. 'Oh, she must have finished, here's the patient now.'

A white-faced man came slowly out of the treatment-room, then stopped and held on to the top of the desk as if for support.

'Would you like to sit down for a few minutes?' Lynne asked kindly. He nodded and walked across to a row of chairs.

June nodded at Frances. 'I think this might be a good time,' she said. They walked out from behind the desk and crossed to the treatment-room, where June tapped on the door.

As they entered, a petite woman in a navy blue uniform turned from an instrument trolley. She was very pretty with small features, china-blue eyes and her blonde hair tied back under her white frilly cap. Her eyes narrowed slightly as she caught sight of Frances.

'Whatever did you do to that poor man, Sandra?' June asked with a chuckle. 'He looked quite ill when he came out of here!'

'He'd had a hernia operation. I only took his stitches out, for heaven's sake. Honestly, men are such babies!' She sniffed, then her gaze flickered back to Frances.

'Sandra, I'd like you to meet Frances Marriott,' said June. 'You were on holiday when she came to see us before. Frances is Dr Ryan's trainee.' She turned. 'Frances, this is Sandra Jones, our practice nurse.'

Frances held out her hand, but the other woman barely touched it, simply nodding in response with no word of welcome. Her attitude took Frances by surprise, for it was in such marked contrast to the behaviour of everyone else.

June went on to query some matter of supplies, and Frances found herself watching the nurse closely. She judged her to be somewhere in her mid-thirties, and closer observation revealed lines of discontent on her face. As she waited for June, Frances remembered that Alex Ryan had told her that Sandra could be difficult, a fact that, now she'd met her, she didn't find hard to believe.

They left the treatment-room, still without a friendly word, and Frances decided that she might well have to accept the situation. She'd done very well up until that point, and she took the attitude that she really couldn't expect to get on with everyone.

The rest of the morning was taken up with more explanations in Reception and a coffee-break in the staff-room, where she renewed her acquaintance with Neville Chandler. The senior partner, a bluff, hearty man in his sixties, couldn't remember who she was at first, but after June had patiently reminded him he proved to be kindness itself. Coffee was followed by a spell with June in her office discussing the doctors' duty rota, then, before she had time to collect her thoughts, the morning had passed and it was lunchtime. She was about to make her way up to her flat for a quick sandwich when Simon appeared in Reception.

'Frances!' He seemed to have recovered from his tiredness and was evidently pleased to see her. 'How about a quick pie and a pint at the Mucky Duck?'

She hesitated but, not giving her a chance to refuse, he took her arm. 'Come on, I mustn't be long, I've calls to make, but I'm not one of the breed of doctors that can go all day without sustenance.'

With a laugh she gave in and allowed him to lead her to the door, where he turned and winked at the girls behind the desk, who seemed to find the whole thing very amusing.

On their way through the car park they met Alex on his way in from an emergency visit. He frowned slightly when he saw them. 'Don't forget our meeting, Frances,' he said briefly.

'Don't worry, Alex, I'll get her back,' said Simon, then with a grin he added, 'The poor girl has to eat, you know.'

With a curt nod Alex walked past them and into the house.

'My God, you'll have to watch him,' Simon muttered as he opened the passenger door of his sports car for her. 'He's a right slave-driver.'

'I can see I'm in for a busy year.' Frances pulled a face as she took her seat. Then, as Simon climbed in beside her, she glanced curiously at him. 'Where did you do your trainee year?'

'Birmingham, a tough inner city practice. It was hell.' He gave a wicked chuckle. 'And I loved every minute of it!'

With a smile she leaned back against the headrest, then, as they pulled out on to the promenade, the fresh sea breeze caught at her hair, whipping tendrils forward across her face, and she gasped with pleasure as Simon put his foot down and the MG surged forward.

Five minutes later they reached the pub, which was crowded with lunchtime tourists and a few regulars. The landlord seemed to know Simon and indicated a small table in a window recess, and as soon as they were seated he brought them a menu.

'What would you like?' Simon looked at Frances, who was studying the menu.

'Oh, just an orange juice, please, and a toasted cheese sandwich. I must keep a clear head for this afternoon.'

'You mean your meeting with Alex?' he asked after he'd ordered a low-alcohol lager and a baked potato and salad.

She nodded. 'Yes, that and my first surgery afterwards.'

'Are you taking it or is Alex?'

'Oh, Alex, thank goodness,' she replied with a shudder.

'Personally, I think that's worse then taking it yourself, it's so boring.'

'That may be so, but at least he won't be breathing down my neck watching every move I make.'

He laughed. 'You don't seem to have a very good impression of Alex yet, do you?'

She shrugged. 'I don't know what's wrong. He seems so abrupt with me, and I feel as if I antagonise him somehow.'

'Don't worry about it, you'll soon get used to

him.' He glanced up at the waitress who had brought their food. 'Hello, Mandy, how are you today?' he asked with a charming smile.

The girl blushed and smiled. 'Hello, Dr Mitchell, I'm fine, thank you.' She spoke with such familiarity that Frances guessed that Simon must be a regular customer at the pub.

As they began eating, he said, 'Now, that's quite enough about Alex. What did you think of the others?'

Frances considered for a moment. 'Well, I like Beatrice.'

'Yes, she's a good sort is old Bea.'

'Is she married?'

He made a noise that was a cross between a snort and a guffaw. 'Bea? Married? Not on your life! Mind you, rumour has it,' he leaned forward and lowered his tone, and Frances noticed a wicked gleam in his eyes, 'that our Bea has always carried a torch for old Neville. Won't have a word said against him, you know.'

'Neville? But he's married, isn't he?' Frances bit into her sandwich, thinking how easy Simon was to talk to.

'Yes, of course he is, and very happily so, I believe. In fact Bea and Sybil, his wife, are the best of friends, but apparently he and Bea go back a long way. Were at medical school together, so I've heard. I should imagine old Bea wishes she'd snapped him up when she had the chance.'

Frances smiled and wondered if she would feel like that about Andrew in years to come. Would she wish she'd snapped him up when she'd had the chance? She glanced up and realised that Simon was still leaning forward and was staring intently at her.

'What is it?' she asked, startled.

'Your eyes—they're the most incredible colour.' He put his head on one side. 'They're not really blue, but, on the other hand, they aren't green either. Can people really have turquoise eyes?'

'You tell me.' Frances laughed, but felt none of the embarrassment she'd experienced when Alex Ryan had commented on her hair.

'Well, it really is the most devastating combination with your dark hair,' he said, then added, 'Is it inherited?'

She nodded. 'Yes, from my mother. She's Irish, and I believe our colouring is quite common in her part of the world.'

'Does she still live there?'

'No, my parents live in Cambridge.'

'Our practice nurse used to live in Cambridge,' he commented, then quite casually he added, 'Have you met Sandra yet?'

Frances nodded, then pulled a face. 'Coming from Cambridge is probably the only thing we have in common,' she said.

'Why? What do you mean?' He threw her an interested look.

'I got the distinct impression she didn't like me.'

'Ah, it wouldn't be you personally she doesn't like.'

Frances frowned. 'I don't understand.'

'It'll be the situation.' He laughed and took a sip

of his lager. 'Don't worry, Frances, Sandra would dislike any female trainee that Alex took on.'

Frances paused, her sandwich halfway to her mouth, and raised her eyebrows questioningly.

'Oh, yes.' Simon nodded, his eyes widening. 'Bea isn't the only one carrying a torch—Sandra's fancied Alex ever since she came to the surgery.'

'And how long ago was that?'

'Let me see, now.' He considered. 'About two years, I think.'

'And is it reciprocated?' She asked the question casually, but when he didn't answer immediately she found herself holding her breath as she waited for his reply. It suddenly mattered very much to her that her trainer wasn't indulging in an extramarital affair.

'Not really.' Simon shrugged, and Frances relaxed, expecting him to make some reference to Alex's wife and family, but instead he said, 'Sandra's his patient, and Alex wouldn't risk anything in that direction. But rumour has it that our Sandra is pretty desperate.'

'It sounds as if I've entered a den of vice,' said Frances with a grimace.

'Not entirely,' Simon replied with a grin. 'Now take me, for example. Fancy-free, quite available, and as long as you don't register with me we could have a ball.'

Frances laughed. There was something irresistible about Simon Mitchell. 'I've already decided to register with Bea,' she said, then seeing his look of delight she added hurriedly, 'and not for the reasons you suggested either.'

He shrugged. 'Well, you can't blame a chap for trying.'

She couldn't help smiling, then glancing at her watch she said, 'I really think I should be getting back, Simon. I daren't be late for my meeting with Alex.'

Draining his glass, he stood up. 'OK, but we must do this often. You can't imagine the difference you've made to my solitary lunch hour.' He winked at Mandy as they passed the bar.

'No,' replied Frances drily, 'I really can't imagine.'

A little later when they drew into the surgery car park Frances suddenly remembered the flowers that had been in her flat and what June had said about them, and as they got out of the car she said, 'Oh, Simon, was it you who put the flowers in the flat for me yesterday?'

He paused and leaned on the roof of the car, staring at her. 'No,' he replied slowly. 'But I wish it had been. Now, why didn't I think of it?'

Frances gave a slight shrug. 'Well, if it wasn't you and it wasn't June, then who could it have been?'

They walked up the steps together and Simon grinned. 'Perhaps it was Neville. He's full of old-world charm.'

'I should hardly think so—he didn't even remember who I was,' Frances replied with a laugh.

'Well, in that case I can't help. Perhaps you should ask Doris; there's very little goes on in this place that she doesn't know about.'

'Good idea.' Frances walked into Reception, then

she saw Alex Ryan standing in the open doorway of his consulting-room. From the impatient look he gave her he was obviously waiting for her, and he didn't appear too happy either.

CHAPTER FOUR

'RIGHT, Frances.' Alex stood back to allow her to enter his consulting-room. 'If you're ready, can we make a start?'

She nodded, but her heart sank at the impatient note in his voice. He closed the door behind them, then indicated for her to take a seat in a chair which he had placed alongside his own.

'The first thing I want to discuss is your training schedule,' he said, sitting down and opening a file on his desk. She waited for him to continue, noticing that he looked tired and that there were fine lines of tension round his eyes that she hadn't noticed before.

'For the first week or so we'll take alternate surgeries—that is, you'll sit in on mine and I on yours.' He glanced at her and she nodded again. She had expected this would happen and Simon had more or less confirmed it. 'Gradually you'll take surgeries alone, and we'll discuss the list after each one,' he continued. 'We'll talk about your rapport with the patient, your diagnosis, your treatment, whether or not you issued a prescription and whether you felt the need to refer the patient to a consultant. Is that clear?'

'Yes, perfectly, thank you,' she replied, trying to sound in control.

'I will of course always be available if you have a problem with a patient, and you mustn't hesitate to ask. One evening a week we'll have a tutorial session. I suggest for that we get away from the surgery environment. You could come to my house.'

It was a statement rather than a question, proved by the fact that he didn't wait for her reply. 'Once a month you'll attend a seminar at the local hospital, where you'll also of course have your weekly day-release sessions with other trainees in the area.'

While he was speaking, although she was listening intently, Frances found herself staring at his hands. Hands always fascinated her, and Alex Ryan's were particularly well shaped, strong-looking but with the right degree of sensitivity that a doctor's hands should possess.

'Now is there anything you wish to ask me?' he finished.

'Yes. . .what about house calls?'

'You will of course be expected to do house calls, but for the time being you'll be accompanied. This also includes night visits.'

'What system do you have for that?'

'We operate a call-forwarding system operated by our local ambulance control centre. They'll ring me if there's an emergency call, then if I think it's one you should attend, I'll ring you and pick you up en route. We carry a bleeper so we can be contacted at all times.'

'I see.' She nodded slowly.

'You sound dubious—is there a problem?'

'I was just wondering how far away you live.'

'A mere stone's throw. Down by the harbour.' As he spoke the phone rang on his desk, and he frowned as he picked up the receiver. 'What is it, Lynne? I did ask not to be disturbed.' He gave a sigh, then a half-smile flitted across his features and once again Frances was struck by how handsome he looked when he smiled and his face lost that dark, brooding look. 'In that case,' he said briefly, 'you'd better put her through.'

Something in the way he spoke suggested to Frances that it was probably his wife on the line, and discreetly she looked away, studying the diet charts on his wall. She couldn't help, however, overhearing what he said.

'All right, my love—I'm sorry too. Tell you what, how about a swim tonight and supper at the Harbour Lights?' There was a silence while he listened to the person on the other end, then he laughed and said, 'I must go now; see you later.'

As he replaced the receiver Frances turned and was struck by the softening of his expression. The tension of earlier had disappeared, apparently dissolved by the making up of some previous argument. For a moment she felt a pang of something that could almost be defined as envy. The proposition of a swim followed by supper had sounded very attractive, and briefly it reminded her of the arguments she'd had with Andrew which had always been quickly followed by a delightful making up.

His next statement, however, rather distorted the romantic image she'd conjured up.

'Teenagers—who understands them?'

'I beg your pardon?' Frances looked bewildered.

He glanced at the phone. 'That was my daughter, Lucy. She's fifteen, and I must confess is far more of a mystery to me now than she ever was when she was five. We had a big row last night because she'd dyed her hair.'

'But don't all teenagers do that?' Frances asked mildly.

'Probably—but I thought three colours at once was a bit over the top! If she returns to school like it after the holidays her headmistress will most likely expel her. She wouldn't listen to reason, though. Everything I say these days she considers to be hopelessly outdated.'

'Can't her mother get through to her?' Frances smiled. 'I seem to remember when I was a rebellious teenager I could wind Dad round my little finger, but I usually took notice of my mum. If I were you I should leave it to your wife to deal with her.'

As she was speaking she noticed a curiously shuttered expression had come over his face, then as someone knocked at the door he said quietly, 'My wife is dead.'

She was attempting to mutter her apologies when Beverley opened the door and placed the bundle of patients' records on the desk for the afternoon's surgery.

'Thank you, Beverley,' he said briskly, and, not giving Frances a chance to say more, he added, 'Send the first one in, please.'

Beverley nodded and left the room, leaving the door ajar.

Still Frances floundered for something to say. Why hadn't someone told her he was a widower, then she could have avoided making such an insensitive remark? In desperation she stole a glance at him and saw to her dismay that he still had the same shuttered expression on his face. Could it be that his wife had died only recently and the very mention of her name was too painful for him to bear? She took a deep breath, but before she had a chance to speak, the first patient of the afternoon tapped on the door and pushed it open.

To her amazement Alex's attitude changed as if by magic, and by the time the patient, a young woman with a tiny baby, had sat down there was a charming smile on his face as he introduced her, then proceeded to enquire about the problem.

It turned out to be a severe case of nappy rash, for which after he'd gently examined the by now squalling baby he prescribed a soothing cream. 'Make sure you cleanse the area thoroughly every time you change Kelly's nappy, Michelle, and try to let the air get to it as much as you can, then, when she's completely dry, apply the cream. If there's no improvement after five days bring her back to see me.'

'Thank you, Doctor.' The young woman, Michelle, began to dress the baby again as Alex washed his hands then issued the prescription on his computer.

'Is everything else all right, Michelle?'

'Oh, yes, thank you, Doctor. Everything's fine

now that Wayne's stopped drinking. We're very grateful for what you did.'

After she'd left the room and before he pressed the buzzer for the next patient, Alex briefly explained to Frances, 'Wayne is her husband. They were married very young, straight from school, in fact, and when she conceived the pressure proved too great for him and he hit the bottle. We got him to accept counselling and it seems to have done the trick.'

'The baby seemed healthy enough,' said Frances, then hastily added, 'apart from the nappy rash, of course.'

'Yes, Michelle does seem to manage her very well, but I think I'll ask the health visitor to call in again.' He scribbled a note on his jotter.

'Would she not go in automatically to such a young baby?'

'Yes, she would. But I happen to know that on each of her recent visits there hasn't been anyone at home. At one point when the father was drinking heavily the baby was considered at risk, so I do want her to make contact again.' As he was speaking he pressed the buzzer for the next patient.

This time it was an elderly man, Mr Richards, who at first looked startled to see Frances, having obviously forgotten that the receptionist had told him that Dr Ryan had a trainee with him. But after it had been explained to him who she was, he seemed to quite like the idea of having an attractive young lady to talk to. From then on he directed all his comments to her, practically giving his medical life history and ignoring Alex, who sat back in his chair with an amused expression on his face and let Frances take over.

Mr Richards was a diabetic, and he had brought with him his medical summary sheet from his latest appointment at the diabetic clinic at the local hospital. He handed it to Frances, who glanced uncertainly at Alex. He indicated for her to continue, and on reading the sheet she found that the consultant had recommended a change in the dosage of his medication.

'Did they tell you at the hospital that you were to take more tablets each day?' she asked, and when Mr Richards nodded she handed the sheet to Alex, who began to alter the directions for Mr Richards's drugs on the computer and issue him with a new prescription. While he was doing this, she enquired if everything else was all right with the patient. He assured her it was now that he'd told her all about it, and happily he took his leave.

As the door shut behind him, Frances felt herself relax.

'That's better,' said Alex, then added facetiously, 'In fact, that's all there is to it!'

She gave a rueful laugh. 'Oh, if only that were so!'

The remainder of the afternoon's list was varied, with routine blood-pressure checks, two asthmatics who needed medication and a middle-aged lady with irritable bowel syndrome. Most of the patients seemed to accept Frances, with the exception of one, and, if Frances had been asked to hazard a guess as to which one it would be, she would have said the elderly man with prostate problems, but in fact it turned out to be a woman of thirty-five who insisted on seeing Dr Ryan in private.

Frances merely smiled and made herself scarce, Alex already having prepared her that something like this might happen. She wandered out into Reception, where she found Lynne busy filling in request forms for cervical smears.

'How's it going?' Lynne gave a sympathetic smile.

'Oh, not too bad. But I think I'm going to be the new girl for a long time.'

'You'll soon get used to it.'

'Lynne,' Frances hesitated, 'how long has Dr Ryan been a widower?'

'Oh, let me see now, it was just before he came here that his wife died. So that must be five years ago.'

Frances stared at her. From the way he'd reacted she'd imagined his wife's death had been much more recent than that. 'Oh, I see. . . Thank you.' She realised that Lynne was looking at her in rather a peculiar way. 'It's just that I didn't know. . . I rather put my foot in it with a flippant remark.'

'He is rather sensitive on the subject; in fact he hardly mentions her at all now. Apparently he adored her.'

'Oh, dear, that just makes me feel worse!'

'I shouldn't worry about it. You weren't to know.'

'I wish someone had told me.'

'Well, as I said, Eloise is very rarely mentioned now.'

Eloise. So that had been her name. 'How did she die? Was it an accident?'

Lynne shook her head. 'No, it was cancer. I understand she underwent a lot of chemotherapy, but it didn't help.'

'There are children, I believe?'

'Oh, yes, two—Nicholas who's about seventeen now and Lucy who's fifteen.' She glanced up as Alex's female patient appeared. The woman's eyes were red and she looked as if she'd been crying. The buzzer sounded and Lynne nodded at Frances. 'You can go back now if you like before I call the next one.'

'OK, Lynne. Oh, and thanks for filling me in.' She went back into the consulting-room and for the rest of the afternoon she felt reasonably satisfied with herself, hoping that she was asking the right questions and sounding sufficiently intelligent when Alex asked for her opinion. Throughout the entire afternoon, however, there was one thought that entered her mind repeatedly. A thought that however much she tried to dismiss it returned with alarming persistence. It was, quite simply, the fact that Alex Ryan was not married.

Towards the end of the afternoon they went upstairs to the staff-room for a tea-break, and as they passed Reception Beverley called out to Frances that her trunk had arrived and had been taken up to her flat by the delivery men. 'Simon was here when it arrived,' she added. 'He was horrified, and disappeared into his room in case he was going to be called on to help again.'

'Our ever-gallant Simon,' observed Alex wryly. 'Charm itself until the going gets tough.'

'Well, I was glad of his help yesterday.' Frances sprang to his defence. 'My cases were jolly heavy.'

Alex made no reply, and Frances was left with the impression that there was slight friction between the two men.

Neville Chandler was in the staff-room, and after he'd kindly enquired how Frances was getting along he said, 'Oh, by the way, my dear, my wife is holding a little supper party on Saturday evening. It's by way of welcoming you into the fold, so to speak.'

'How kind!' Frances flushed with pleasure.

'Who's on call on Saturday?' asked Alex as he poured their tea.

'It's Bea's weekend on,' replied Neville. 'She says she'll carry her bleeper, drink non-alcoholic wine and keep her fingers crossed. You'll be there, of course, Alex?'

'Try keeping me away.' Alex smiled. 'Neville's wife, Sybil, is the best hostess in town,' he explained to Frances.

She merely smiled in response, suddenly unable to speak, for her heart had given a crazy little leap of pleasure at the news that Alex was to be present. It would be nice to see him socially. Her hopes were dashed however by Neville's next remark.

'We've asked June and her husband and Sandra, of course, if they would like to join us.'

Frances glanced quickly at Alex to see his reaction to the fact that the practice nurse would also be there. His expression remained inscrutable, however, and she found herself wondering if there was indeed any truth in the rumours that Simon had spoken of. At the time she'd thought the main obstacle to any relationship with the nurse was that Alex was married—that, and the fact that she was apparently his patient. But, as Frances had now discovered, Alex was a free man, and according to Simon Sandra was pretty desperate.

Her thoughts chased each other round and round in her head as she sipped her tea. Then suddenly she pulled herself up sharply. What in the world was she thinking of? She'd just ended one relationship, for heaven's sake—the last thing she wanted was another. She couldn't deny the fact that she'd found Alex Ryan attractive from the very moment she'd set eyes on him, but he was at least thirteen years older than she, she'd only known him for a couple of days and, even more important than that, he was her trainer for the next year, and any sort of relationship on those lines would surely be frowned upon as it could only interfere with her tuition.

Leaning forward, she set her cup and saucer down on the coffee-table, then taking a deep breath she resolved to herself that from that moment on she would put any such notions concerning Alex Ryan right out of her mind.

As she looked up, however, she became suddenly and uncomfortably aware that he was watching her. Not watching her casually but studying her intently.

She felt the sudden rush of colour to her cheeks and glanced at Neville as if for support, but he had his nose buried in a medical journal. Helplessly she transferred her gaze to the window and the sea scene beyond, unable to look at Alex immediately for it was as if he had read her thoughts, stripped her mind naked and was analysing her most intimate feelings.

When at last she felt able to look again in his direction he had finished his tea. Jumping impatiently to his feet, he said abruptly, 'This won't do—we still have the extra patients with emergency appointments to see.'

With a quick smile in Neville's direction she followed Alex from the staff-room, only too aware once again of his abruptness of attitude towards her. Was it simply that he found her irritating, or could it be something deeper than that? She wished she knew, for she felt it could inhibit their working relationship. There had been something unnerving about the way he had been staring at her, something intensely intimate about his expression, and then barely seconds later had come that brusque, abrupt manner that she was certain he wouldn't even adopt with a complete stranger.

It was perplexing, and Frances found it still occupied her thoughts after surgery had ended and she climbed the stairs to her flat. She prepared herself a meal of soup, a cheese salad and some fresh fruit, and then began the task of unpacking her trunk, something to which she had been looking forward ever since she had heard it had arrived.

Together with her reference and medical text-books she had several well-loved novels, her music cassette player and favourite tapes, a few pictures and posters and several brightly covered cushions, all of which would help to stamp her personality on the flat.

Last but by no means least she lovingly unpacked her precious collection of cats, arranging them on shelves and at strategic spots throughout the flat. She had started the collection when she was a child and it had steadily grown over the years, in fact to such an extent that she was no longer able to take the entire collection around with her. A large china cabinet at her parents' home in Cambridge housed the remainder, but her favourites went with her.

Finally satisfied, Frances stood back and admired them: cats in china and brass, in wood and the finest porcelain, cats of all types and breeds, cats from Thailand, from Egypt and Burma, royal cats and homely British tabbies, they were all there, helping to make the flat feel more like home.

Hearing a sound outside, she opened the door and found Doris with her hand raised just about to knock on the door.

'Hello, love,' said Doris in her friendly fashion. 'I just came up before I go home to see if you're all right.' She looked past Frances into the flat. 'Have you got all you want?'

'Oh, yes, thanks, Doris, I'm fine,' Frances replied happily. 'I've just been unpacking my trunk and arranging my collection of cats. Look, do you like them?' She stood back, and Doris stepped into the sitting-room.

'Oh, I say, don't you have a lot! I'm actually a dog

person myself, but I must say they're very nice. How did your first day go, dear?'

'Not too bad, Doris, although it all seems a bit strange at first.' Frances smiled, then added, 'Everyone's been very kind, though, and I do appreciate it. . .which reminds me, Doris do I have you to thank for those beautiful flowers that were here to welcome me yesterday?'

Doris had turned and was about to go down the stairs, but she paused at Frances's question with one hand on the banisters and looked back. 'You mean those lovely roses and freesias?'

Frances nodded.

'Oh, no, dear, it wasn't me, I only found a vase and arranged them. It was Dr Ryan who brought them for you.'

CHAPTER FIVE

FRANCES rose very early the following morning, and leaving the house by the back entrance through the tiny walled garden she went for her swim. It was another bright, clear summer's morning, but the sun, although well above the distant horizon, was only hinting at the warmth to come. The sea was cold, and Frances gasped at the icy first touch, then with a deep breath she plunged straight in.

She had been relieved when she walked down the beach that this morning there was no sign of Alex either in the water or in the vicinity of the surgery. Somehow she felt she wanted a brief respite from him, if they were to spend each and every day together.

She struck out with a strong crawl stroke, releasing a pent-up surge of energy and tension until finally, invigorated, she flipped over on to her back and floated, staring up at the vast expanse of sky.

It had come as a shock when Doris had told her that the flowers had come from Alex. He had been the last person she would have expected to send them, and he must have wondered why she hadn't taken the trouble to thank him. She found herself confused by his motives, however. No doubt they had simply been meant as a welcoming gesture, a gesture she found touching, but he had made that gesture before she'd arrived, and it seemed to Frances that ever since he'd set eyes on her she'd sensed his hostility.

She couldn't imagine why, and found herself wondering if it was that he resented having a trainee in tow. But it couldn't be that. No one forced him to take on trainees, and when he had come to the hospital she had been struck by his apparent enthusiasm. Maybe she was just imagining it all and his abruptness was simply part of his manner.

She made up her mind that she would try to see if he was the same towards the other members of the staff, but she knew that the one thing she would have to do without any further delay was to thank him for his flowers.

When at last she set back towards the shore she found herself scanning the beach, and when she saw it was deserted she hated herself for the stab of disappointment she felt. However much she might have tried to delude herself that she was pleased Alex hadn't come for his early morning swim, she knew that deep down she had subconsciously been looking for him.

Later, however, after she'd showered and dressed, this morning discarding her office suit in favour of a flame-coloured full skirt and white shirt, she found that all her fears and apprehensions were back at the prospect of taking her first surgery with Alex as an onlooker.

June Ritchie was in Reception and she looked up with a smile as Frances came down the stairs. 'Good morning, Frances. So you survived your first day. Well done! Nothing will seem quite so bad now.'

'Don't you believe it,' Frances replied darkly. 'I've got my first surgery this morning.' As she spoke she glanced towards Alex's consulting-room. The door was shut, and looking at June she added, 'Is he in yet?'

June nodded. 'Yes, he's reading his mail. He said for you to go in when you came down.'

'Thanks, June.' Taking a deep breath, Frances crossed Reception and tapped on Alex's door.

He was engrossed in a letter and barely looked up as she came into the room, merely muttering a greeting and waving vaguely for her to take a seat.

She sat quietly for several moments, trying to interest herself with the various posters on the walls, but failing miserably as her concentration drifted and her gaze kept returning to the man behind the desk. This morning he was dressed in a light grey suit and a navy shirt, and apart from his abruptness, to which by now she was becoming accustomed, she thought he looked less tired and drawn than he had the day before.

Almost as if he sensed her scrutiny he suddenly glanced up, their eyes met and their gaze held for several seconds before Frances, in confusion, looked away.

Suddenly he thrust a sheaf of letters across the desk. 'You'd better have a look at these,' he said tersely. 'These people are your patients as well now. You'd better familiarise yourself with them.'

It was almost an order, somehow implying that

Frances had been sitting back doing nothing, and she felt the colour rise to her cheeks as she took the papers and began to look through them.

They were mainly reports, blood tests, thyroid function tests, X-ray results, pregnancy tests and letters from consultants, but they meant nothing to Frances, who knew none of the patients.

She tried to look intelligent and to show interest, aware that Alex was watching her, then quite unexpectedly she saw a name that she recognised, and with a start she realised she was holding the MSU result of the patient she had gone to see with Alex the previous morning.

Carefully she read the report. 'I'm glad to see I was right,' she said quietly as she passed the form back across the desk to Alex.

He nodded, but his expression gave nothing away. 'We will visit her again this morning. What will you recommend?'

'That she continues with the antibiotics I prescribed and that we will review the situation when she's had her X-ray,' Frances replied firmly, but she suddenly had the uncomfortable feeling that he had given her the reports deliberately to see if she would spot the MSU among them.

'Right.' He stood up. 'Shall we go?'

'Go?' She looked bewildered. 'Isn't it time for surgery?'

'It is.' He looked faintly amused. 'But, as it's your surgery, don't you think we should go to your room?'

'Oh. . .oh, yes, of course.' She scrambled to her

feet, trying to collect her case and gather up the papers he'd thrust at her, then hurriedly she followed him from the room and down the short passage to the back of the house and her own consulting-room.

She felt self-conscious as she took her seat, this time behind the desk, while Alex took his place slightly behind her and to one side.

Beverley had already placed the morning's set of patient records on the desk, but Frances knew that by rights she should also use the computer screen. It was already switched on, and as she turned towards it she hesitated, for although she'd used one at the hospital, each system was different.

It was Alex who came to her rescue, reading the details on the first set of notes and typing the number on to the keyboard. As the patient's particulars flashed up on the screen he seemed to sense her nervousness and gave her one of his rare smiles.

Instead of calming her, however, which was what he had surely intended, it simply set her pulses racing, and as she pressed the buzzer her hands felt clammy.

Taking a deep breath she sat up straight and, smoothing the dark glossy strands of her hair behind her ears, she adjusted the stand-up collar of her shirt, only too aware of Alex's eyes upon her. Just when she felt she was unable to go another second without meeting his gaze she heard a tap on the door.

'Come in,' she said, and her voice faltered slightly, then as her first patient entered her room she made a supreme effort to focus her concentration one hundred per cent on what she was doing.

The morning seemed to pass in a whirl, but as Frances grew more confident she found herself enjoying it. Her main problem seemed to arise from the fact that most of the patients were registered with Alex and understandably chose to address their remarks to him rather than to her.

One middle-aged lady, however, presented Frances with a multitude of symptoms and, just as she was wondering where she should start, Alex intervened and casually asked the woman how long it was since her husband had died. Immediately Frances knew she was dealing with a case of delayed grief and was able to treat the patient accordingly, concluding her advice with a suggestion of bereavement counselling.

After the patient had gone Frances gave Alex a grateful look. 'Thanks for that,' she said.

'You have to bear in mind that in general practice you have to deal with the patient as a whole,' he explained carefully. 'Not just with symptoms but with family and background. It will be very different from your work as a houseman, where you will have concentrated solely on the symptoms and treating the complaint.'

Frances sighed. 'I feel at such a disadvantage—you know these people and everything about them. To me they're all strangers.'

'You'll get to know them, believe me, and if it's any consolation I felt exactly as you do when I first started in general practice. Oh, and Frances,' as

Alex continued she glanced up sharply, 'try and relax a bit more—you seem rather tense.'

He smiled at her again and for a moment she could detect no trace of his former abruptness and hostility. On a sudden impulse, she said, 'I believe I owe you an apology, Alex.'

'You do?' He raised his eyebrows in surprise.

'Yes, I had no idea it was you I had to thank for the lovely flowers that were waiting for me in my flat when I arrived.'

He shrugged and for a brief instant she thought he seemed embarrassed. 'It was the least I could do. Damn it, that flat was cheerless enough.'

'Oh, I've improved things immensely,' she said. 'In fact, I've become quite fond of my little abode in the heavens.' Then impulsively she added, 'You must come up and see.' When he didn't reply, she thought she'd overstepped the mark again and blundered on, 'Anyway, I really appreciated the flowers. . .'

'Don't you think we should get on?' Quizzically he indicated the buzzer.

'Oh. . .oh, yes, of course.' She felt the colour touch her cheeks again, but she also felt a little surge of happiness for she believed that just for a moment they had shared a moment of rapport. Maybe it was a good omen for their future working relationship, she thought, as a young girl opened the door, walked sulkily into the room and slumped down into the chair.

She could have been no more than sixteen, and

her lank, dirty blonde hair fell into her eyes partly concealing a spotty complexion.

Frances glanced at her records. 'Hello, Sarah,' she said. 'I see you're a patient of Dr Lloyd's, but she's away today. My name is Dr Marriott. How can I help you?'

The girl didn't answer immediately, glancing suspiciously at Alex from beneath her hair, then with a noisy sniff she said, 'I thought I was seeing Dr Lloyd.'

'As I explained, it's her day off,' Frances replied patiently. 'Now do you feel you could tell me what's troubling you?'

Still the girl hesitated, then Alex stood up. 'I'll just go and collect those records from Reception while you're having a chat with Sarah,' he said firmly, and before either of them could reply he had gone, shutting the door tightly behind him.

Frances immediately sensed the easing of tension in her patient and kindly she said, 'Now, perhaps we can talk?'

At last the girl nodded, then said bluntly, 'I haven't come on.'

'How late are you?' Frances asked gently.

She shrugged. 'I didn't come on last month—nor this time either. I'll have to get rid of it,' she added flatly.

'Don't you think it might be a good idea if we were to find out if there's anything there first?'

The girl shrugged again. 'I know there is, and there's no point you trying to talk me into keeping it, because I won't!'

'Sarah, at this point I'm not going to talk you into anything. It may be a false alarm. Your periods could be late for any number of reasons.'

'I've never missed before,' the girl replied, but as she tossed her hair back in a gesture of defiance Frances noticed the glint of tears in her eyes.

'Well, we must find out for sure.' Frances opened a drawer, took out a specimen pot, then took down a form for a pregnancy test from the rack behind her desk. 'I want you to do a sample of your water first thing tomorrow morning. Bring it into Reception with this form and give it to one of the girls at the desk. We'll send it off to the hospital for testing and we should have the result back in twenty-four hours. Whatever the result is, Sarah, I shall want to see you again.'

'Like I said, I'll have to have an abortion. My mum would kill me if she found out!'

'What about your boyfriend?'

Sarah hesitated, then bitterly she replied, 'He weren't my boyfriend. It happened on the works outing. He's married to one of the girls in the packing department, so, like I said, there's no way I could keep it.'

Frances took a deep breath and tried not to show any reaction. 'Well, Sarah, let's make sure first, shall we? Then we'll discuss it afterwards.'

The girl nodded curtly, then stood up and with barely a backward glance left the room.

Alex returned almost immediately. 'I thought it better to make myself scarce.' He glanced at his watch. 'In actual fact she was the last, so I suggest we go up for coffee.'

Frances nodded and together they left her consulting-room and went upstairs to the staff-room.

As they drank their coffee Alex casually asked if she'd had any problem with the girl, Sarah White.

Frances shook her head. 'Not at the moment, but there may be when her pregnancy test comes back.'

'Hmm, I thought it might be that. How old is she?'

'Sixteen, and she's saying that, if it's positive, there's no way she's going through with it.'

'What about the lad?'

'He's hardly that. He's married, and it sounds as if it was a one-night stand.' Frances looked thoughtful for a moment, then said, 'Alex, I know Sarah is Beatrice's patient, but do you think she would let me see the case through?'

'I'm sure she would. Bea is very reasonable.' He threw her a shrewd glance as he replaced his cup and saucer on the table. 'Why? Do you feel you can handle it?'

'I don't know, but I'd certainly like to try.'

'Good for you.' He smiled encouragingly. 'And good luck—I've a feeling you'll need it. Teenagers can be so unpredictable.'

Frances looked up quickly. 'Talking of teenagers, what happened about your daughter's hair?'

He pulled a face. 'Well, we finally reached a compromise. It's still dyed, of course, but at least it's only one colour now.'

Frances laughed, thinking how different he seemed when he relaxed. 'Ah, but which colour? Green?'

He stood up and held open the door for her. 'Not quite. No, it's not that bad, it's a sort of. . .' He hesitated, and as she passed him in the doorway she paused so that they were very close, almost touching.

'How about burgundy?' she suggested as she caught a sudden scent of his aftershave, a tangy citrus smell that instantly appealed.

'Burgundy. . .?' he mused. 'Yes, I suppose you could call it that. But how did you know?'

She laughed as he followed her down the stairs. 'Oh, it wasn't that difficult to hazard a guess. I'm not that far removed from today's youth, you know.' As she spoke she turned her head and looked back at him, and was just in time to see his expression change and the shuttered look come into his eyes that she'd seen once before.

He didn't answer and, wondering what in the world it was she could have said to bring about such a sudden change of mood, she watched helplessly as he went off to his room to collect his case for the day's house calls.

Their first call was on the patient whom they had seen the previous day. They found her comfortable and responding to treatment, so Frances left instructions for her to continue with the medication for five days, by which time she should have received her X-ray appointment.

'When your X-ray result is back we'll want to see

you again, so you'll need to make an appointment at the surgery,' Frances explained.

As they were driving to their next call, Frances stole a glance at Alex. Whatever it was that had happened to bring about his sudden change of mood was still very much in evidence; his jaw was set, his dark brows were drawn together in a frown and he remained silent.

Frances sighed and turning away looked out of the window. They had driven to the far side of the town, an area she hadn't seen before, an area of blocks of flats with a rather run-down feeling.

The patient they had come to see, an elderly man, lived on the fifth floor of one of these tenement blocks. He suffered from angina and chronic bronchitis aggravated by a lifetime of smoking. The lift in the flats was out of order, and as they climbed the stairs Alex explained the patient's history to Frances, adding that he had resisted all Alex's attempts to curtail his smoking.

'It'll kill him in the end,' he said as they reached his flat. 'But he knows that and, in a way, he accepts it.'

The man, Mr Buckley, seemed to be living in a degree of squalor that shocked Frances. His bedcovers were filthy, piles of newspapers littered the floor and the remains of a meal were on a table by his bed.

After Alex had examined him he asked if Mr Buckley wanted him to arrange for meals on wheels.

'No.' The old man shook his head. 'I had them

before.' He coughed noisily, trying to clear his throat. 'I don't like them.'

'So what do you do about your food?'

'I've got Ada, downstairs; she gets me fish n' chips.'

'All right, Mr Buckley, if you're happy with that. But I'm going to arrange for a district nurse to come in to see you.'

'What for?' Immediately the old man looked suspicious and plucked agitatedly at his bedclothes.

'She'll bring your medicine and make you more comfortable,' Alex replied, and his tone invited no further resistance.

After they'd left and got back to the car, Frances said, 'Wouldn't someone like Mr Buckley be better off in residential care?'

'Better off for whom?' Alex raised his eyebrows. 'For him, or for those having to look after him?'

'For him, of course,' Frances replied tersely.

'But he's quite happy where he is. Moving him would only make him miserable.'

'But surely. . . I mean for his health. . .'

'His health would deteriorate even further if he were miserable,' Alex replied firmly. 'I'm all in favour of keeping these old folk in their own homes whenever possible, providing, of course, that's what they want.'

Alex remained in the same withdrawn frame of mind for the rest of the morning's house calls. It was so far removed from the brief rapport they had shared earlier in the day that Frances was relieved when they returned to the surgery and Simon once again whisked her off to the pub for lunch.

He was his usual exuberant self and was all agog to hear how her first surgery had gone.

'Well, I don't think I disgraced myself,' she said slowly, looking up from the menu. 'But I'm still finding Alex rather hard going.'

'In what way?' Simon looked sympathetic.

She hesitated. 'I'm not sure; it's nothing I can put my finger on, but I seem to say things that irritate him.'

'I believe a lot of trainers treat their trainees like students to begin with,' Simon replied, then as the waitress approached he smiled at her and waited as Frances ordered. It wasn't Mandy, but he seemed to know her equally well, and laughed and joked as he ordered his own lunch.

After she had gone Frances said slowly, 'It isn't really that. I can't say he treats me like a student. I think the problem's more on a personal level.' Simon looked surprised, and she frowned, then added, 'I seem to keep saying the wrong thing.'

'How do you mean?'

'Well, for a start, I didn't know he was a widower, and I made some flippant remark about his wife.'

'That was hardly your fault, he can't blame you for that.' Simon leaned forward. 'Don't you think you could be over-reacting a bit—you know, ultra-sensitive in a new job?'

She shrugged. 'I don't know, maybe I am at that. Probably it's all in my imagination.'

Their food arrived at that moment and the subject

was forgotten, then as they were nearing the end of their meal Simon said, 'Are you going to this bash at Neville's on Saturday?'

She nodded. 'Yes, are you?'

'I suppose so.' He sighed. 'Although I can think of better ways of spending a Saturday night. Still, if you're going, it'll be better. Maybe we could slip off to a disco or a club if the going gets too heavy.'

She laughed. 'I can hardly do that, Simon—after all, it's supposed to be in my honour. Besides, I understood that Neville's wife is supposed to be an excellent hostess.'

'That's right, she is.' He brightened up at the thought. 'She makes the most delicious sweets.'

'Well, there you are, then. . .it won't be too bad.'

He pulled a face. 'It's just the prospect of having to endure a whole evening of Bea simpering at Neville, Sybil pretending not to notice and Sandra making cod's eyes at Alex.'

Frances felt a pang at the mention of Alex's name in connection with that of the practice nurse.

Simon, however, carried on, unaware of her reaction. 'Still, as I said, now that you're going, it'll make all the difference. Who knows, I might even find myself looking forward to it! Tell you what, I'll pick you up on Saturday night about seven-thirty. Then no one will think anything of it when I say I'm taking you home, and maybe we just might manage a late drink somewhere. How about that?'

He looked so eager that she had to laughingly agree with his suggestions, but as they drove back to the surgery she couldn't help wishing that it had been Alex who had offered to take her to the Chandlers'.

CHAPTER SIX

FRANCES found herself taking a great deal of care over getting ready for the supper party on Saturday evening. She wasn't sure why she was taking so much trouble, neither did she want to examine her motives too closely.

Friday had followed much the same pattern as the two previous days, with Frances sitting in on another of Alex's surgeries and vice versa. It had been just as they were clearing up at the end of the day that he had asked her how she was getting to the party.

She had hesitated before replying just long enough for him to say that he would call for her. She had then, of course, been forced to say that Simon had already offered to take her.

Alex had merely shrugged, but Frances had found herself wishing desperately that she could change the arrangements.

Simon had made it very plain that he would also be taking her home, just as he was making it increasingly obvious that he would like there to be more to their relationship.

After she'd showered, Frances stepped into a camisole of beige lace, the sheerest of stockings, and then took from its hanger the dress she'd chosen to wear. It was plain, black and silky, in a soft loose style with very narrow shoulder-straps. Its simplicity

accentuated her slim figure, and the plain gold
jewellery she wore showed off her creamy colouring
to perfection. With a touch more make-up than
usual and a light mist of her favourite French per-
fume, she was finally ready.

Simon was waiting for her in Reception, and the
look in his eyes told her what she already secretly
knew—that she was looking her best.

'Dr Marriott, you look sensational,' he commented as he helped her into his car. Mercifully she
noticed that tonight the hood was up. 'Are you sure
you want to go to old Neville's? With you looking
like that we could paint the town red!'

'Oh, dear, are you implying I'm overdressed for
the Chandlers' party?' She glanced at him in dismay.

'Not at all, just wasted. No, Frances, don't you
worry, the women will all be dressed up to the nines,
but believe me, you'll outshine the lot of 'em.' With
a wicked chuckle he put his foot down and they
roared off, taking the main road out of the town.

The Chandlers lived in a quiet tree-lined avenue,
the foliage partly concealing the individual mock-
Tudor properties. As Simon pulled on to the drive
Frances noticed several other cars were already
parked. Bea's battered old Citroën was wedged
between a red BMW and a dark blue Volvo. There
was, however, no sign of Alex Ryan's Audi.

They were greeted by Sybil Chandler, an elegant,
charming woman of around sixty who ushered them
through the hall and lounge and on to the patio
where the rest of the guests were enjoying drinks in
the coolness of the soft summer's evening.

Bea, resplendent in bottle-green velvet, was standing on the lawn beside a willow tree which dipped its branches into a picturesque lily pond. She was in animated conversation with a tall, ascetic-looking man who turned out to be a local solicitor, a bachelor, and a lifelong friend of the Chandlers.

It soon became apparent to Frances that on this occasion he had been invited to balance the numbers, just as it became obvious that she had been paired with Simon. June Ritchie was accompanied by her husband, and Sandra Jones had apparently come with them.

Only Alex hadn't arrived, and Frances couldn't help but notice how Sandra's eyes constantly strayed towards the house as if she was waiting for him to appear. Tonight the petite blonde looked quite exquisite in a cyclamen-pink cat-suit, but she had greeted Frances in her usual cold manner with a false smile that didn't reach her eyes.

Everyone else, however, had seemed delighted to see Frances, and Neville, in his usual hearty manner, had hailed her as the guest of honour.

'So how's it all going, then?' Bea had abandoned her solicitor and was bearing down on Frances and Simon, who quickly extricated himself and went off to talk to June. 'I don't seem to have seen very much of you this week, I'm afraid,' she boomed in her usual forthright fashion.

Frances smiled. 'It's been a bit confusing, but I think I'm slowly sorting everything out.'

'Good show! Alex told me you saw one of my girls

a couple of days ago. Want to see the case through, I hear?'

'Yes,' said Frances quickly. 'I would like to, with your permission of course.'

'Certainly, but one word of advice. The girl's family aren't such ogres as she might paint them.'

'Thank you, Beatrice,' Frances replied gratefully. 'I'll remember that. . .' She paused as the older woman looked past her and her expression suddenly changed.

'Ah, here he is. . .' she murmured.

Frances turned sharply and almost spilled her drink. Alex Ryan was standing with Sybil in the open doorway, his dark head bent, and while he was obviously listening to what she was saying he was staring across the terrace to where Frances was standing with Bea.

Her eyes met his and for a split second she could have sworn his expression was one of surprise. Their glances held, locked together for a moment suspended in time, a moment where it seemed as if they were alone, as if the other members of the party ceased to exist. Then it was gone, people moved, voices carried in the still air, and as Sandra moved swiftly forward to claim Alex's attention Frances was left wondering if she had imagined it.

Supper was served in the dining-room, around a large oak refectory table, in the soft light of candles set in silver candelabra and with the french doors open to the fragrant night.

Frances was seated on Neville's right with Simon on her other side. Both men kept her entertained with very different types of conversation, but throughout the evening she was constantly aware of Alex.

He was seated further down the table, with June and Sandra on either side. Even at a distance it was evident that Sandra monopolised him, almost ignoring Dennis, June's husband, on her other side.

Simon had been quite right in his assessment of Sybil's role as hostess, however, for the food was quite superb, and gradually as the evening progressed Frances felt herself unwind. Between Neville's hilarious anecdotes of his forty years in general practice and Simon's acerbic wit as he gave a discreet running commentary of the proceedings, she felt herself really relax for the first time since she'd arrived at Pebblecoombe.

At one point the conversation around the table became general as someone asked after Alex's children, and Frances found herself listening intently for his reply.

'Nick is studying for his A Levels,' Alex replied. 'He takes them next summer, but he'll need high grades if he's going to do what he's set his mind on.'

'Still determined on becoming a vet?' Neville asked from the head of the table.

Alex nodded. 'Yes, as far as I can remember he's never wanted to do anything else.'

'And what about your daughter?' asked Dennis Ritchie.

Alex hesitated. 'Ah, well, Lucy's another matter entirely,' he said wryly, but with a smile.

'Still stage-struck, is she?' asked Bea with a laugh.

'You know, Alex, if I were you, I'd encourage her. With her looks she could become a Hollywood star.'

'I know,' he replied grimly. 'That's just what I'm afraid of.'

In the general laughter that followed, Frances noticed that Sandra leaned closer to Alex and whispered something in his ear. She saw him laugh in reply and wondered what it took to make him laugh in that relaxed fashion, just as she wondered so many other things about this man whom she hardly seemed to know at all. In fact, she thought ruefully as she sipped her wine, she had probably learnt more about his family in the last five minutes than she had in the whole of the last week.

Bea was called out once after the main course but, as she was back in time for dessert, it was generally decided she'd got off lightly.

It wasn't until they had adjourned to the lounge and were sitting in the deep leather armchairs drinking coffee that Frances was reminded of Simon's intentions for the rest of the evening.

He was perched on the arm of her chair, and as he leaned forward to place his cup on a low table he murmured, 'Do you think we could soon make a decent exit?'

She glanced up and for the umpteenth time that evening her eyes met Alex's across the room. She looked quickly away, then at her wrist-watch. It was nearly midnight.

'I would think everyone will be going soon,' she replied quietly. 'But I don't think I should be the first to make a move.'

At that moment Alex stood up and looked towards his hostess. 'May I use your phone, Sybil?'

'Of course, Alex, you know where it is,' she replied.

As he left the room Simon grinned at Frances. 'Look at Sandra getting edgy,' he said softly. 'She came with June and Dennis, but you can bet your boots she's hell-bent on Alex taking her home!'

Frances glanced at the blonde, who indeed seemed to be fidgety as she waited for Alex to come back.

'You've got to hand it to her,' Simon chuckled, 'she's a trier. Do you know what I heard yesterday?'

Frances shook her head, but for a moment she dreaded what she might be about to hear.

'She's re-registered with Bea, so there's nothing to stop any relationship between her and Alex now.'

Frances barely had time to recover from the sudden pang she felt at Simon's words before Alex came back into the room and everyone looked up.

He turned to Sybil. 'I'm afraid I shall have to ask you to excuse me, Sybil. One of my patients started early labour this evening. It's a home confinement and one I'd promised to attend; I've just phoned the midwife and it looks as if it's going to be an interesting case, so if you can spare her, I should like Frances to come with me.'

He looked at Frances as he finished speaking, and she felt her heart give a sudden jump.

Sybil, who was well used to such sudden changes of plan having been married to a GP for nearly forty years, nodded understandingly, but as Alex and

Frances made their farewells the look of fury on Sandra's face was only too obvious.

On Simon's handsome features, however, the expression of disbelief was almost comical, and Frances found herself unable to meet his gaze.

It was with a definite sense of relief that she almost collapsed beside Alex in the Audi. As he switched on the ignition he threw her a look that was almost sardonic.

'Do I detect that you're as pleased as I to be able to make a legitimate exit?' he asked.

She took a deep breath. 'You could say that.' She leaned back against the headrest, then glanced quickly at him, wondering if he might have misinterpreted her remark.

His classic profile, clearly visible in the moonlight that flooded the quiet street, remained inscrutable.

'I don't mean that I didn't enjoy myself,' she said quickly. 'I did, and the Chandlers are lovely people, but. . .'

'But there were one or two undercurrents you found heavy going,' he finished for her.

She hesitated, unsure how to answer. 'Yes,' she replied at last, 'something like that.'

They drove in silence for some while, and Frances wasn't sure whether it was the effects of Neville's excellent wine but she suddenly felt a tremendous sense of well-being. It seemed totally right to be beside Alex Ryan in his car in the middle of a soft summer's night.

Almost as if he sensed her mood he leaned forward and flicked the switch of the cassette player.

Immediately the car was filled with the romantic sound of a classical guitar.

She glanced at him again and he, sensing the movement of her head, took his eyes from the road and looked at her.

'You look lovely, Frances,' he said softly. 'You outshone every other woman there. They aren't used to competition.'

She smiled. Simon had said the same thing. At the thought of Simon, she started guiltily, for she had more or less indicated that she would go for a drink with him.

Almost as if he guessed her thoughts, Alex said, 'Did you and young Mitchell have anything lined up for after the party?'

'Sort of—we had talked of going on somewhere, but I'm sure he'll understand. After all, when duty calls. . .' She broke off as a sudden possibility hit her. 'We really are going to a confinement, aren't we?'

Even in the darkness she sensed his shocked expression. 'Of course we are! Whatever did you think? That I was abducting you?'

Frances felt her heart flip over at the very suggestion of being abducted by Alex Ryan, of being carried off somewhere by him and of having him make wild passionate love to her. Then sternly she checked the erotic thoughts that had suddenly threatened to go right out of control. Whatever was wrong with her? Alex was quite simply her trainer and they were on their way to a night visit.

As they approached the patient's house through

the darkened streets Alex briefly gave Frances a history. It was Lorraine Janes's second baby. Her first, a girl, had also been born at home, and Alex had been present on that occasion. The mother was of the comparatively rare Rhesus-negative blood group, and that, together with the fact that the midwife had informed him that the baby was in the posterior position, was enough for Alex to want to keep an eye on her at the birth.

The door was opened to them by the patient's mother, a Mrs Wilson, who seemed delighted to see Alex again.

'Dr Ryan!' she exclaimed. 'How good of you to come!' Her gaze flickered to Frances, taking in the way she was dressed. 'Is this your wife? It looks as if baby has disturbed your evening.'

'Not at all,' Alex laughed as Mrs Wilson stepped aside and they entered the hall. 'Babies have the habit of arriving when they're ready, not to suit anyone else—and no,' he turned to Frances, 'this isn't my wife, this is Dr Marriott, a trainee GP attached to our practice.'

'Oh, I see. Well, come on upstairs. Sister Parry is with my daughter. Apparently the baby is still in the wrong position, but Sister says there's still time for that to right itself.'

In the bedroom they found everything under the strict but calm control of Sister Parry, the community midwife. The mother-to-be, Lorraine, appeared happy and relaxed, and it was her husband who seemed to be suffering from agitation.

Alex introduced Frances, and Peter, Lorraine's

husband, seemed relieved that there were to be no fewer than two doctors in attendance on his wife.

'The baby's not in the right position, you see, Doctor,' he explained to Frances.

'So I believe,' she replied gently. 'But there really isn't anything to worry about, Mr Janes. All it means is that the baby is probably going to arrive face upwards instead of downwards. It isn't really a complication, you know.'

'That's what I keep telling him,' Lorraine said wearily, 'but he won't believe me.'

'It may mean that the baby may take rather longer to arrive,' said Alex. 'So perhaps it would be a good idea if you were to go and make some tea, Peter. Don't worry, we'll give you a shout if anything starts to happen.'

Peter Janes did as he was told, and Mrs Wilson went off to find an overall for Frances, for as she said, 'We can't have Dr Marriott getting that beautiful dress in a mess, can we?'

The labour progressed without incident, the baby not rotating and remaining in the posterior position, but as predicted it took rather longer than usual. It was nearly four o'clock when Sister Parry announced that the patient's cervix was ten centimetres dilated and she could feel the anterior fontanelle.

'It's definitely a "face to pubes" delivery,' she said, 'but the foetal heart is fine.'

By this time Peter Janes was by his wife's side, offering encouragement during the second stage of labour.

After a word with Sister Parry, who was to

actually deliver the baby, Alex told Frances he wanted her to give an 0.5mg injection of Synometrine to Lorraine. By this time Lorraine's labour and everyone's waiting was being rewarded as the baby's head was born.

The crown of dark hair was the first thing Frances saw, quickly followed by the tiny scrunched-up face, then as the anterior shoulder emerged she administered the injection necessary to prevent haemorrhaging during the third and final stage of labour.

As Baby Janes finally pushed his way into the world it was Frances who, at a sign from Sister Parry, gave the news to the delighted parents that they had a son.

The slightly unusual labour had resulted in a small tear, and after the delivery of the placenta Alex indicated that Frances would be responsible for applying the sutures. First, however, while the midwife took a sample of blood from the placental cord for grouping, Frances took a larger sample of maternal blood, which as the patient was Rhesus-negative would go for testing. If the baby proved to be Rhesus-positive the mother would need an Anti-D injection to prevent her developing antibodies in her blood which could endanger any further pregnancies.

While Lorraine Janes cuddled her new son Mrs Wilson brought in more tea for everyone, then, after Frances had put in the few sutures that were required and Sister Parry had bathed and weighed in the baby at a healthy eight pounds, a sudden commotion at the door made them all turn.

A tousle-headed little girl stood in the doorway, rubbing her eyes.

'She woke up and couldn't wait to see her new brother,' explained her grandmother, and as Peter Janes lifted his little daughter up into his arms and approached the bed, Alex touched Frances's arm.

'Time we were gone, I think,' he said quietly.

She nodded, and they would have slipped quietly out but Lorraine called out to them. 'Thank you, thank you both for helping to deliver Alexander,' she said.

Frances glanced at Alex and was in time to see some indefinable emotion flit across his features.

Outside in the car they sat silently for a few moments, and he made no attempt to start the engine.

'It sounds as if you're rather special to that little family,' Frances said softly.

He shrugged slightly. 'Lorraine had a rough time when Charlotte was born, and I promised her I would be present for this one as she particularly wanted a home confinement.'

'Do you think she should have gone into hospital?'

'I think it's every woman's right to have the choice,' he said firmly, then as he reached forward to start the ignition he said, 'You did very well in there, Frances. Even Jo Parry seemed impressed. Have you done much time in obstetrics?'

Frances smiled in the darkness. 'Hardly any.'

'You didn't let it show. Well done.'

It was the first time he had ever praised her, and she felt a warm glow inside.

'Are you desperately tired?' he asked casually as they drew away from the Janeses' house.

'No—I feel wide awake,' she replied, not adding that in fact the baby's birth had left her feeling exhilarated and very far from sleep.

'In that case let's go and watch the sun rise over the sea,' he replied.

At his words Frances felt a thrill flutter the length of her spine, and with a little sigh she sank back into the soft grey leather upholstery of the Audi.

CHAPTER SEVEN

Alex took the road that led to the cliffs, finally stopping the car on a vantage-point that overlooked the town, the bay and the small harbour beyond the headland.

The sky was already lightening to a pearly glow, while the town below lay swathed in a dawn mist. He switched off the engine and they sat for several moments without speaking. It was Frances who finally broke the silence.

'I always think there's something very moving about a child being born just before dawn,' she said quietly.

'The very miracle of birth never fails to amaze me,' Alex replied. 'Each time I witness it, it's as if it were the first. It always makes me feel humble, as if nature were cutting us down to size, telling us that however much we might progress she will still have the last word.'

Frances turned her head and looked at him curiously, almost with a sense of wonder at this sudden revelation of his innermost thoughts. It seemed so out of character, just as this evening he had acted towards her without his usual abruptness and hostility, giving her hope that their relationship might have taken a turn for the better. As she studied his profile an overwhelming sensation flooded over her, and suddenly she felt it was as if she had known him all her life.

Almost as if he were reading her thoughts he turned and looked at her, their eyes met in the cool dawn light, each acknowledging the signals they had been exchanging throughout the night, and in a purely spontaneous gesture he slipped his arm around her shoulders.

The sun had just tipped the distant horizon, transforming the pewter-grey of the sea to iridescent beauty. It rose gradually like a great silent orb, pale and golden as if stripped of its fire; with a sigh of contentment Frances leaned against Alex's shoulder.

They watched in silence for a long time, and it was Alex who moved first; gently he ran the fingers of one hand through her glossy hair. He caught his breath, and with a sound that could have been a sigh or a stifled groan he reached out his other hand, his strong fingers cupping her jaw and tilting her face towards him.

Wonderingly she stared into his eyes as he eagerly searched every feature, his gaze finally coming to rest on her mouth. She held her breath, hardly able to believe that this was happening after his aloofness towards her. She couldn't convince herself it wasn't a dream until she felt the touch of his lips in a kiss that started as the merest contact, once again causing the delicious fluttering down her spine.

When she offered no resistance, the pressure of his mouth became more insistent, and she finally found herself responding with a sudden surge of desire and her lips parted beneath his. With his

Free Books Certificate

Yes! Please send me my 4 Free Medical Romances, together with my Free Glass Dishes and Mystery gift. Please also reserve a special Reader Service subscription for me. If I decide to subscribe, I shall receive 4 superb new books every month for just £5.80, post and packing free. If I decide not to subscribe, I shall write to you within 10 days. The free books and gifts will be mine to keep in any case.

I understand that I am under no obligation whatsoever - I can cancel or suspend my subscription at any time simply by writing to you.
I am over 18 years of age.

Extra Bonus

We all love surprises, so as well as the Free books and Glass Dishes here's an intriguing mystery gift especially for you. No clues - send off today!

3A1D

Mrs/Miss/Ms _____
(BLOCK CAPITALS PLEASE)

Address _____

_____

_____ Postcode _____

Signature _____

Reader Service
FREEPOST
PO Box 236
Croydon
Surrey
CR9 9EL

NO STAMP NEEDED

Send No Money Now

hands entangled in her hair, his kiss became more and more urgent as if he were demanding the surrender of her very soul.

She had no idea how long it lasted; it might have been seconds or equally it could have lasted an eternity. For Frances time had stood still, for quite simply never before had she been kissed like that. When at last he literally tore himself away she found she was shaking.

'This is madness,' he muttered as he turned from her and seemed to be struggling for self-control. 'I'm sorry, Frances—it shouldn't have happened, but quite honestly I've been fighting the urge to do that all night.'

'There's no need to apologise, Alex,' she replied softly.

He shook his head and sitting up straight reached for his seatbelt. 'No, I took advantage of a situation, and in our circumstances it was unforgivable.'

He seemed to have completely missed her implication that it had been what she too had wanted and she stared at him in dismay, wondering how she could tell him.

He gave her no chance, however, switching on the engine and reversing the car away from the cliff-top, seemingly oblivious now to the glorious scene before them as the sun's hue had deepened to a rich gold, sending streaks of fire across the sea.

As they drove away Frances felt her heart sink. Had that kiss meant nothing to him? Had it merely been a temporary lapse on the part of a lonely man? She stole a glance at him, but he was tight-lipped.

Surely, she reasoned, it couldn't just be that he was lonely? It was only too obvious that Sandra Jones was desperate for his company, so why had he driven her, Frances, to this lonely spot to see such a romantic sight as the sun rise over the sea when all along he had behaved so abruptly towards her?

That she was strongly attracted to him she could no longer deny, in spite of the fact that she had tried to convince herself that she wanted no romantic involvement. There had been something about Alex Ryan that had stirred Frances almost from the moment she'd set eyes upon him, and until now his almost hostile indifference had only seemed to fuel her interest.

The closeness they had shared that night, followed by the kiss, had for a moment caused her to thrill at the thought that he too might be caught up in a situation of mutual attraction.

Now, however, she wasn't so sure as he drove at high speed through the deserted Sunday morning streets.

They travelled the length of the promenade, and when they reached the cul-de-sac she half expected him to screech to a halt outside the surgery and throw her out of the car.

But he didn't. In fact, he didn't even enter the cul-de-sac, and when she turned to him she was surprised to see a half-smile on his face.

'Come home to Harbour Reach and I'll cook you breakfast,' he said.

'No, really, there's no need. . .'

'It's the least I can do in the circumstances,' he

murmured. Something in his tone invited no further argument, and Frances fell silent, biting her lip at the realisation that once again he seemed to be not only apologising for what had happened but feeling he had in some way to make amends.

Suddenly the urge to set the record straight was too much for her, and as they turned into Harbour Road she said quickly, 'Alex, about just now. . . I don't want you to think. . .that is. . .'

He brought the car to a halt in front of an old stone house that seemed to guard the very entrance to the harbour and turned to her. 'I don't think anything of the sort, Frances. As I said, it should never have happened, and I can assure you, you needn't worry about our future working relationship because I won't let it happen again.'

'No,' she intervened quickly, struggling for the right words, 'you don't understand. You see, when I came here I'd made up my mind I didn't want any sort of involvement——'

'And ever since you've set foot in the place you've had young Mitchell pestering you and, as if that weren't enough, tonight you've had me to contend with as well. I should think between us we constitute a case for sexual harassment! I can only apologise again, Frances, and if you wish I'll have a word with Simon, because I have the feeling he's really keen, and I know he can be persistent.'

'Oh, please, no——'

'The thing is, Frances, you are an exceptionally lovely young woman. We know little about you, and what we've probably all overlooked is the fact that you no doubt have another commitment. Am I right?'

He smiled, but she thought she sensed a flash of pain behind the glibness of the question. She hesitated, causing him to prompt her for a reply.

'So I was right? There is someone special?'

'Well, there was. . .'

'Ah, another doctor?'

'Yes, we were at medical school together, but——'

He gave her no chance to explain, opening his door and climbing from the car, and by the time she had joined him he had changed the subject and was pointing out the view across the harbour.

'It's beautiful, isn't it? I don't think I could ever bear to move away from this house. It's quite unique; I'd never find another like it.'

Uneasily Frances turned and followed him into the house, uncomfortably aware that somehow he had ended up with entirely the wrong impression, but uncertain how she could now put things right. If she went to great lengths to tell him her relationship with Andrew was over would it imply that she would welcome Simon's attentions? Suddenly she was confused, and realised at the same time that tiredness was rapidly catching up with her.

The house was very old and, as Alex explained as they quietly let themselves in the front door, it had for many generations been the home of the current harbour-master.

As Alex closed the door a cat suddenly appeared, rubbing itself around their legs by way of greeting.

He was black with a white bib and four white paws, and Frances exclaimed in delight as she fondled him.

'Oh, but he's beautiful!' she exclaimed, then, smiling up at Alex, she said, 'I didn't somehow imagine you to be a cat person.'

'Misty's not really mine,' replied Alex. 'He belongs to my daughter Lucy.'

The house had been lovingly restored, cleverly incorporating its old-fashioned charm with every modern convenience. The gound floor was almost entirely open-plan, with impressive sea views from each of the many high windows. A huge stone fireplace with an open hearth dominated one wall, while to one side a wrought-iron spiral staircase wound its way upwards.

The furniture too was old, a rich mahogany dining suite and a dresser filled with an exquisite gold-patterned dinner service, while the sofa and deep armchairs matched the floral tones of the curtains. Many fine antique maps and paintings adorned the rough-textured white walls, and Frances couldn't refrain from exclaiming in delight at the overall effect.

Alex smiled and removed his jacket. 'You like it, then?'

'Yes, very much,' she replied as she studied a painting of the Battle of Trafalgar. 'It's different.'

'I'll start the breakfast,' he said, heading towards the far end of the vast room which obviously housed the kitchen area. 'If you'd like to freshen up, it's first left at the top of the stairs.' He nodded towards the staircase.

'Thank you, I would.' Frances was suddenly aware of how she must be looking. She crossed the room and cautiously climbed the stairs.

The house was quiet, and Frances assumed that Alex's family must be sleeping for it was still very early. She found the bathroom and was pleased to rinse her hands and face, apply a little fresh make-up and run a comb through her tousled hair. As she recalled how her hair had become tousled, she blushed and for a few seconds she rested her hands on the washbasin and, staring at her reflection in the mirror above, allowed herself the luxury of reliving those precious minutes.

She was still in a trance-like state when she left the bathroom but, as she shut the door behind her and turned, she was jolted back to reality by a figure that leaned against the banister rail, arms folded, eyeing her with suspicion.

'Oh, you made me jump!' Frances gave a little gasp, quickly followed, as she recovered, by a smile as she saw the mass of deep burgundy-coloured hair, a great chunk of which was screwed into a bunch high on the side of the girl's head. 'You must be Lucy,' she said, adding quickly, 'I hope I didn't wake you.'

The girl was incredibly beautiful, but her tiny pointed face and huge dark eyes were marred by an angry scowl as she continued to glare at Frances, obviously taking note of her black evening dress.

Suddenly Frances realised that it must indeed look very odd to this girl that she should be here, in her father's house, so early on a Sunday morning, and dressed as she was. Realising that some sort of explanation was called for, she took a deep breath and, holding out her hand in a friendly gesture, she said, 'I'm Frances Marriott, your father's trainee. . .' She trailed off as the girl ignored her outstretched hand, instead bending down to stroke the cat, who had bounded up the stairs at the sound of voices and was rubbing himself around his young mistress's legs.

'He's a very handsome fellow, isn't he?' Frances too crouched down as the cat transferred his attentions to her. 'Hello, Misty,' she said as he lifted his head and purred in ecstasy as she tickled him beneath his chin.

'His name is Mistoffelees.' It was the first time the girl had spoken, and her tone was unmistakably frosty.

Frances looked up at her. 'Oh, I'm sorry—I didn't know. Your father called him Misty.'

At the mention of her father the girl glanced first along the landing, then over the top of the spiral staircase. 'Where is he—my father?'

Frances swallowed. 'He's downstairs, cooking breakfast. . .we've only just come in.' When the girl's eyes again narrowed suspiciously, she added hastily, 'We've been to a home confinement.'

'But he wasn't on call. I waited up for him after Dr Chandler's party. I wouldn't have done if he'd been on call.'

'It was a confinement he'd promised to attend,' replied Frances, then checked herself. There was no way she was going to justify either her own or Alex's actions to this rather stroppy young woman. At that moment, a strong, delicious aroma of grilled bacon wafted up the stairs. Lucy once again glanced down the stairs as if she was going to go down, then abruptly she seemed to change her mind and, picking up the cat, disappeared into a bedroom, shutting the door firmly behind her.

Frances stared at the closed door for a moment, then with a shrug she went downstairs.

Alex had removed his tie, unbuttoned the neck of his shirt and turned back his cuffs. He looked casual and relaxed, and he smiled at Frances as she appeared in the kitchen area.

'Strictly speaking I'm not really a cooked-breakfast man,' he explained. 'But Sundays, I must admit, are the exception. There's nothing better than a full breakfast, an endless coffee-pot and the papers.'

'What about the early morning swim?' Frances asked the question innocently but with a touch of mischief in her voice.

He looked contrite. 'Ah, I have to confess, even that goes by the board on a Sunday. Sundays have always been the one day I try to unwind and forget everything, unless I happen to be on call, of course, then I keep very irregular hours.'

'Lucy waited up for you last night because she knew you weren't on call,' said Frances casually.

He had turned back to the grill and was arranging tomatoes in the pan, but at her words he turned sharply. 'Lucy? But how do you know that?'

'I saw her just now, on the landing. I got the

impression she thought we'd been out together all night.'

'Which of course we have.' He laughed, then added, 'Don't worry, I'll sort Lucy out. I'm afraid when she's here in the holidays, she gets rather possessive where I'm concerned.'

'I did try to explain, but I don't think she believed me for one moment.' Frances grimaced, then turned at a sudden noise from the front door as the Sunday papers thudded on to the mat. 'In fact, I couldn't get anything right. I thought you said her cat's name was Misty?'

'It is.' He paused from serving the bacon on to the plates and frowned at her, then as realisation dawned he laughed. 'Don't tell me, I know. She told you the cat's name is Mistoffelees—right?'

'Right.' Frances pulled a face.

'I forget that's his name—it's such a mouthful the rest of us call him Misty, but Lucy has always stuck to his real name. Her mother took her to see *Cats* when it first opened in the West End and she had the kitten as a present soon afterwards.' As he was speaking, he set the plates down on the breakfast bar, indicating for Frances to take a seat on one of the high stools.

Then, pouring freshly percolated coffee into two attractive pottery mugs, he sat down opposite her. 'Lucy has always been fascinated by the theatre,' he explained. 'And everything in her life has to have theatrical connotations.'

'Didn't I hear you say earlier that she wanted to make it her career?'

He nodded, then paused with his fork halfway to his mouth. 'Yes, she does.'

Something in his tone made Frances glance up. 'And you don't approve?'

'It's too precarious,' he said firmly. 'I've told her, it's fine for a hobby but not as a career. Do you know, she's even got some hare-brained idea of giving up her schooling now and going to some stage school? She hasn't even sat any exams yet, for God's sake!' He was silent for a while as he thoughtfully ate his breakfast, then he continued, 'I just wish she'd take a leaf out of her brother's book.'

'He's going to be a vet? Is that right?'

Alex nodded. 'Yes, Nick has always known what he wanted to do, there's never been any doubt.'

'But hasn't Lucy as well?' said Frances quietly. When Alex looked up in surprise she continued, 'You said yourself she's always been fascinated by the theatre, so it suggests the inclination has always been there.'

He remained silent for a moment, toying with his knife, then standing up he crossed to the percolator and poured more coffee. 'Lucy has a rebellious streak in her, and I think it would do her good if she were to get herself a steady career.'

'Did you have anything in mind?'

He shrugged. 'Well, she's a very bright girl. I would have thought perhaps banking or. . .' He hesitated.

'Or medicine?' Frances raised her eyebrows. 'Could it be, Alex, that you're disappointed that she's shown no inclination in that direction?'

He didn't answer immediately, but when he turned back with the mugs of fresh coffee there was a tight expression on his face. 'I can see that you're set on taking Lucy's part in this, so maybe it would be better if we changed the subject?'

Frances shrugged, but an amused expression played about her lips at the thought that Alex believed he was in danger of being outmanoeuvred.

'As you wish,' she said, taking the mug. 'But what I was really thinking was that I should be getting home.'

'Of course, you must be tired, and you have a full week ahead.'

'I do?'

'Yes, we must get down to your proper schedule. Tuesday you'll have a training day at the hospital and Wednesday evening we'll have a tutorial session here.' His face had taken on the animated expressin he generally wore whenever he discussed work and, as Frances watched him, she wondered if she could possibly have dreamt what had happened earlier. That it had been a mistake on his behalf and that he had never intended it should happen she had no doubt, but still she wondered why he had allowed it to happen.

He drained his mug and setting it down on the breakfast bar he said, 'If you'll excuse me for a few minutes, I'll take some coffee up to Lucy and make my peace with her, then I'll drive you home.'

He poured another coffee then crossed to the staircase, pausing on the way to pick up the newspapers and returning to give them to Frances.

'Have a look at these while I'm gone,' he said.

She watched him as he strode across the room and lightly mounted the stairs, and her breath caught in her throat. If only. . .if only, she thought, once again allowing her thoughts to run riot as she fantasised what could have followed if he had meant that kiss to happen. When her thoughts began to border on the erotic, she gave herself a little shake in an endeavour to pull herself together. She knew she really had to stop thinking of Alex in that way, but at the same time she wished she knew what his true feelings were towards her.

With a sigh she opened one of the Sunday supplements and tried to concentrate on an article about the Royals, but found it impossible. Instead she resorted to flicking through the pages of the magazine, idly glancing at the advertisements. One for porcelain took her eye, and she studied it eagerly, hoping there might be a new cat figurine to add to her collection.

So intent was she that she didn't hear a door open at the far end of the kitchen, and it wasn't until she heard a smothered exclamation that she realised someone else had come into the room. She glanced up sharply and found a woman gazing at her with an expression of shock on her face. She was about sixty, small and wiry with salt-and-pepper-coloured hair screwed back into a bun.

Her hands were covering her mouth as she continued to stare at Frances in astonishment.

'Hello. I'm sorry, did I startle you?' Frances asked in a friendly fashion.

The woman leaned back against a worktop. 'Aye, you did, and that's a fact,' she said in a strong Scottish accent.

Frances smiled. 'It's quite all right,' she said, 'I'm not a burglar. I'm Frances Marriott, Dr Ryan's trainee.' The woman still continued to stare at her, and Frances began to feel uncomfortable.

'I didna think you were a burglar. . .'

'You look as if you thought I were a ghost!' said Frances with a laugh in an attempt to lighten the situation.

The woman, however, made not even an attempt at a smile, but continued staring at Frances in a sort of horrified fascination.

'Aye,' she muttered at last, 'maybe I did at that. Sitting there like that with your fringe falling forward I thought you were Eloise come back.'

Frances caught her breath. 'Eloise?' she asked slowly, but even before the woman had a chance to answer her mind had raced ahead, something clicked and she knew what the answer would be.

The woman nodded, and as she took her hands from her mouth Frances saw they were shaking. 'Yes, you're the image of her, or rather the way she was when she first met Dr Ryan.'

CHAPTER EIGHT

ON MONDAY morning Frances sat at her desk staring at the slip of paper that June Ritchie had just handed to her. It was the pregnancy test result for Bea's patient, Sarah White, and it confirmed the girl's worst fears.

Picking up the intercom, Frances rang through to Reception and asked Lynne whether the girl had made an appointment to see her. Lynne told her that she had and would be coming later. Frances was in fact sitting in on one of Alex's surgeries that morning, but she knew that he would allow her to see the girl alone. She sighed and sat back in her chair, still staring at the scrap of paper which was to change a young girl's life, and she hoped she would be able to handle the case in a way that would be satisfactory to all concerned.

Glancing at her watch, she realised it was high time she joined Alex, but at the same time she knew she was putting it off for as long as she could. She hadn't seen him since he'd brought her home the previous day and, tired as she had been, she had found it incredibly difficult to sleep as her mind churned over and over, analysing what the woman in Alex's home had said to her. She hadn't known who the woman was, because she had gone upstairs

110

before Alex had returned, but on the drive home she'd casually enquired as to her identity.

'Oh, that's Jeannie Cameron,' Alex had said with a smile. 'I didn't realise you'd met her. She's our treasure.'

When Frances had looked at him questioningly, he'd continued, 'Jeannie was a distant relative of my late wife. She came to look after things when my wife became ill and she's stayed ever since. I don't know how we'd manage without her.'

He'd said no more, and Frances couldn't bring herself to mention what the woman had said to her. Maybe it would have been better if she had, but she had remained silent, and for the rest of the weekend it had troubled her. Although it had come as something of a shock hearing that she so resembled his wife, the more she thought about it, it also answered a lot of questions. It explained Alex's comments about her change of hairstyle, the reason she had caught him on several occasions staring intently at her, but, most important of all, it seemed to explain her attraction for him which had been so puzzling in the light of his previous hostility.

It also, of course, had provided a reason for his kiss. A kiss which she had hoped had been for her sake alone but which she now knew had been, on his part, a fantasy of the woman he had once adored.

Her only consolation was the fact that Jeannie Cameron's remark had come in time to prevent her making a fool of herself and telling Alex that she enjoyed his attentions. She had so nearly done so and now, at the very thought of it, she went hot with embarrassment.

Finally she had come to the conclusion that in future the best thing she could do was to keep Alex Ryan at arm's length, not to let him think that she had felt any attraction for him, and to conduct their relationship in a purely professional manner.

It had been with these intentions uppermost in her mind that she had started work, but when she eventually plucked up the courage and went along to Alex's room, she learnt how easy it was for the best-laid plans to go awry. As she opened his door and he looked up at her, her heart flipped crazily and her throat went dry.

Somehow she managed to get through the morning, which proved to be extremely busy with a surgery of very mixed ailments ranging from dyspepsia, acute rhinitis and a duodenal ulcer to a woman with a severe case of pelvic inflammatory disease which had to be referred to a gynaecologist.

Alex seemed quite relaxed towards her and there was no mention of the incident on the cliffs, but Frances endeavoured to put her plan into operation in spite of her treacherous feelings and remained cool towards him. Only once did he register surprise at her manner, when he asked her opinion on a case and she kept her answer so brief and to the point that it sounded curt. After that, it was almost as if he sensed the way she wanted to play things and reacted accordingly by cutting any unnecessary chat and keeping strictly to the matter in hand.

Once she felt a pang of regret for it seemed as if,

having just got the relationship on to a friendlier level, she had immediately destroyed it. Then she dismissed the thought. There was no way she wanted his attentions if he only found her attractive because she reminded him of his wife.

She took her mid-morning coffee with Bea, who was full of grumbles about the hectic Sunday she'd had on call. The tourist season was at its height and the hotels and holiday camps were full, putting enormous pressure on the local GPs. This fact was further brought home to Frances after coffee when Alex asked her to take a temporary residents' surgery with him sitting in.

The surgery was filled with the usual ailments that followed a hot weekend with clear skies and an offshore breeze. Frances saw one case after another of sunburn, severe in some cases, especially where young, fair-skinned children had been exposed to the harmful rays with little or no protection. She found her role to be as much one of educator as prescriber in these cases and, after one particularly severe case that involved a baby whose cheeks were so blistered and swollen that he could scarcely open his eyes, she voiced her anger first to the young father and then, after the family had left, to Alex.

He listened impartially to her outburst then, when she'd finished, she glared at him indignantly. 'Don't you agree with me?' she demanded.

'Of course I do, but I don't believe getting angry helps in these cases,' he replied calmly. 'I think advice, quietly given, is far more effective, as anger only aggravates the situation.'

She bit her lip and pressed the buzzer for the next patient. It seemed she'd got it wrong again.

The surgery continued with other seasonal-related cases: hay fever, summer colds, prickly heat rashes and a few incidents of diarrhoea and vomiting. Then, as the last patient left, Beverley put her head round the door.

'No more TRs,' she said, 'but there's a medical rep to be seen, and Sarah White has turned up an hour late for her appointment. Are you still prepared to see her, Frances?'

Frances nodded and stood up. 'Yes, of course. I'll take her down to my room, if you don't mind, Alex?'

'No, you carry on,' he answered. 'I'll see the rep. Show him in, Beverley.'

Frances found Sarah in the waiting area of Reception. Huddled in a chair, she was staring moodily at the tropical fish in the aquarium. At her greeting the girl started and looked up sharply.

'You're very late for your appointment, Sarah,' said Frances firmly. 'But, now that you're here, perhaps you'd like to come along to my room,' she added, picking up the girl's records from the counter where Beverley had placed them.

With her hands thrust into the pockets of the light jacket she wore over her T-shirt and tatty jeans, the girl followed Frances down the passage.

In her consulting-room Frances pulled her chair round so that she was seated on the same side of the desk as Sarah, so removing any actual or psychological barriers. As they both sat down she couldn't help noticing that the girl's previous display of bravado had disappeared and at that moment she looked just like any frightened child.

As Frances took the pregnancy result from the record envelope she took a deep breath before delivering the news. She was prevented from speaking, however, as Sarah suddenly looked up through her lank hair.

'I was right, wasn't I?'

Frances swallowed. 'Yes, Sarah,' she replied calmly. 'You were right.'

She saw the girl flinch, then defiantly she tossed her hair back. 'I knew I was. I told you I was, didn't I?'

'Yes, Sarah, you did.' Frances paused, then added, 'Now, we have to talk.'

'Nothing to talk about. Like I said, I don't want it.'

'It's not quite that simple, you know, Sarah.'

'Yes, it is—I know loads of girls who've had it done.'

'That may be so, but there must have been a very good reason for their terminations.'

'Well, isn't there a good enough reason for mine?' she demanded, and her eyes flashed.

'I don't know,' said Frances firmly. 'But that's what we need to talk about.'

Sarah gave an exaggerated sigh and began chewing on a piece of gum which she seemed to have kept hidden in her mouth up until that point. 'It's like I said before, it was a one-night stand. He's married with two kids of his own.'

'He may be prepared to take responsibility if he knew about the baby,' Frances suggested.

The girl threw her a withering look. 'You jokin'? He don't take much responsibility for the kids he's got, let alone another one. Besides, I know him, he'd never admit it to his wife.'

As she listened, Frances found herself wondering what a young girl could have seen in such an unsavoury character in the first place, but she knew it would be useless to ask. Instead she said, 'Well, it does rather sound as if we can rule out any help from that quarter, so perhaps we should think about some other options.'

'What options?' Sarah, who had been looking bored, suddenly narrowed her eyes suspiciously.

'There are plenty of married couples who are unable to have children of their own who would dearly love to adopt a baby. These days, there are very few babies around for adoption, so——'

'Hang on a minute!' Sarah sat up straight and glared angrily at Frances. 'Are you suggestin' I lump this kid around for nine months just to make a present of it to someone I don't even know?'

'It was just a thought——'

'Well, you can forget it. Like I told you before, I want to get rid of it, and if you won't help me then I'll find someone who will!' Angrily she jumped to her feet and turned towards the door.

Frances realised she had to act fast if she was going to save the situation. 'Sarah, please sit down!' Her voice had lost the calm gentle tone she had adopted up until then and had taken on a firm authoritarian note.

The girl stopped with one hand on the door-handle and, when she turned, her face registered surprise at Frances's change of tack. Slowly she sat down again and waited for Frances to continue.

'There is one other possible solution to your problem which we haven't yet considered,' said Frances, pausing just long enough to notice a flicker of interest which was quickly replaced by Sarah's habitual expression of rebellion. 'Tell me, Sarah, who do you live with? Your parents?'

'Yes, but I know what you're going to say, and you can forget anything like that. My mum would kill me, and if she didn't my dad would. My sister got herself pregnant, so they've been through it all once.'

'And what happened with your sister?'

'She married him eventually, but they've split up now and she's back home with the baby—well, he's a toddler now.'

'I see.' Frances tried not to smile as she noticed a very slight softening of the girl's attitude as she mentioned her young nephew, but she began to feel more sure of her ground.

'Anyway, I know my rights, and I don't even have to tell them at home if I don't want to—I'm over sixteen,' Sarah finished triumphantly.

'You're quite right, of course, but have you thought how you're going to keep it from them?'

She shrugged. 'Like I said, I'll get rid of it, then they'll never know.'

'And in the meantime? These things take time to arrange, and your mother may guess.'

'Then I shall move out,' she declared.

'Right. Now let's see, Sarah, where did you say you worked? Oh, I know—the paper factory, wasn't it? I wouldn't imagine you earn a great deal there, do you?'

The girl remained stubbornly silent.

'Not enough to get a place of your own, I shouldn't think.'

'I know what you're tryin' to do,' said Sarah. 'You're tryin' to talk me out of it—well, it won't work.'

'Sarah, please listen to me. I'm not trying to talk you into or out of anything. I am simply trying to show you that there are other options to the one you thought was the only one.'

The girl remained silent, gnawing at the side of her thumbnail, then at last she looked at Frances. 'You think I should tell my mum, don't you?'

'I think that would be a very good start. I also think it would be a good idea if we were to talk again, but this time with your mum as well.'

The girl looked up quickly, and through a sudden shine of tears Frances saw a glimmer of hope. 'Would you tell her. . .my mum, I mean? Would you tell her for me?' There was almost a pathetic eagerness about her now where before there had only been defiance.

'Of course I will, if that's what you want,' replied Frances briskly. 'I'll give her a ring and ask her to come in. Do you want to be present, Sarah, when I tell her?'

The girl shook her head quickly.

'Very well, in that case I'll speak to you both again later. Now, Sarah are you feeling a bit better about things?'

The girl shrugged in a nonchalant manner, but Frances felt that in a small way she had got through to her.

After her patient had gone, Frances sat for some moments thoughtfully staring at the phone, then at last she reached out and, lifting the receiver, she dialled the number shown on the front of the girl's records.

A woman answered the phone, and after Frances had established that she was speaking to Sarah's mother she identified herself and asked the woman if she could come into the surgery that afternoon to see her.

She was still pondering on the case and agonising that she was handling it the right way when Alex appeared in the doorway.

'How did it go?' He seemed genuinely concerned.

Frances gave a slight shrug. 'I'm not sure. Ask me again after I've spoken to the girl's mother.'

'I take it you've been landed with breaking the news?' He raised his eyebrows and Frances nodded ruefully.

'Afraid so, but it was my own fault. Still, if it does some good, it'll be worth it.'

'Where do you stand on the abortion issue?' he asked curiously.

'I believe there's a place for it, of course,' Frances answered slowly. 'But I also happen to believe far too many are performed when an alternative solution could be worked out. I did a stint in day theatre during my training and saw my fair share of terminations. I can't say it was a happy time, and of course there are always the long-term psychological effects to consider which these young girls can know nothing about.'

Alex nodded. 'I'm glad we feel the same way about that issue, at least,' he commented drily, then he disappeared back to his own room leaving Frances wondering about his cryptic remark.

She spent the remainder of the morning catching up on some paperwork, then at lunchtime she made her way out to Reception, wondering if Simon was anywhere around. They had fallen into the habit of taking their lunch together, but today there seemed to be no sign of him. June was in Reception talking to Lynne and she glanced up as Frances approached.

'June, have you seen Simon?' asked Frances.

'Simon? No, it's his day off.'

'Oh, so it is. I'd quite forgotten.' Frances was thrown for a moment as she'd been hoping to see Simon to apologise for leaving him in the lurch on Saturday night.

'Were you supposed to be having lunch with him?' asked June curiously.

'Oh, it's not exactly a permanent arrangement,' explained Frances. 'We just go to the pub if we both happen to be free.'

'Well, how about having a sandwich with me instead?' asked June in a friendly way.

'Love to, but tell you what, why don't you come up to the flat with me—you haven't seen it since I moved in, have you?'

'Great; I have one phone call to make and I'll be with you.' June made her way to her office just as the treatment-room door suddenly opened and Sandra appeared with Alex close behind her. He had his dark head bent as if he was listening to something she was telling him and they were both laughing.

Frances watched them as they crossed Reception and went out of the front door then, as Alex opened the passenger door of his car and Sandra slipped into the seat, she felt a pang of some emotion she could only describe as jealousy. Quickly she turned her head away, not wanting to see more, but she was in time to catch the knowing look that passed between Lynne and Beverley.

She was soon joined by June, however, and was given no further time to speculate whether Alex was merely giving Sandra a lift somewhere or whether he was taking her to lunch.

As she climbed the stairs in front of June she reprimanded herself. After all, it had been her decision to keep her relationship with Alex purely professional, so she only had herself to blame if he showed interest elsewhere.

June was amazed and full of admiration for the way in which Frances had transformed the rather bare little flat into a warm, colourful apartment where one felt immediately at home.

They settled down to coffee and sandwiches, and inevitably the conversation turned to practice gossip.

'Did you enjoy yourself on Saturday night?' June asked casually, and for a moment Frances panicked, thinking she had somehow found out about the time following the confinement, but then she realised to her relief that June was simply referring to the supper party.

'Oh, yes, very much,' she answered hastily. 'Neville and Sybil are such a lovely couple.'

'Yes,' agreed June, 'and it was so nice to see Alex so relaxed. We don't see nearly enough of him socially.'

'Did you know his wife?' Frances suddenly found herself asking.

June shook her head. 'No, she died before they moved here. She was very beautiful, I believe, although Bea tells me that she lost her looks and all her hair during her illness. I saw a photograph of her once a long time ago. Alex used to keep one in the drawer of his desk.' She paused and sipped her coffee, then threw Frances a sharp glance. 'You know, of course, that Sandra fancies her chances with Alex?'

Frances swallowed. 'Yes, I had heard a rumour. Do you think she'll get anywhere?' She asked the question as casually as she could, but she found herself holding her breath as she waited for the other woman's reply.

'I sincerely hope not. She's completely wrong for

Alex, not his type at all, but then who can tell?' She sighed. 'There's no accounting for taste, and you know what they say about gentlemen and blondes.'

During the afternoon Sarah's mother came for her appointment with Frances. Alex was taking the surgery but, as arranged, he went out of the room so that Frances could see Mrs White alone. She was in her late thirties, overweight to the point of obesity and neatly if shabbily dressed. She also had a very anxious expression.

'I've been that worried, Doctor, since you phoned. It's about Sarah, you said?'

Frances nodded. 'Yes, it is, and Sarah knows that I've asked you to come and see me.'

'So what is it, Doctor?' The woman began twisting a paper tissue in her agitation. 'What's wrong with our Sarah?'

'There's nothing really wrong with Sarah. . .'

'Then what. . .?'

'Your daughter's pregnant, Mrs White. I arranged for a pregnancy test to be done and we had a positive reply this morning.'

The woman was staring at her with a curious expression on her face. Frances cleared her throat. 'I'm very sorry, Mrs White, but——'

'Expecting, you say?'

'Yes.'

'And there's nothing else wrong with her?'

Frances shook her head, bewildered now by Mrs White's reaction.

The woman gave a great sigh of relief. 'Well,

thank God for that! I didn't think you'd get me down here to tell me that. I thought. . .well, I don't know what I thought. I was imagining all sorts. . .cancer. . . AIDS. . . But pregnant!'

'Well, I'm sorry if I've put you through any unnecessary anguish,' said Frances, amazed that the woman seemed relieved about her daughter's condition. 'Am I right in believing that you don't think Sarah's pregnancy is going to be too great a problem?'

The woman shrugged in a resigned sort of way. 'Well, these things happen, don't they? It won't be the first time in our family and I don't suppose it'll be the last. Did she tell you who the lad was?'

'She did. He wasn't exactly a lad, Mrs White, and there isn't going to be any wedding. He's already married.'

'Silly little cow. She's going to get the sharp edge of my tongue later, I can tell you! What does she think she's going to do about it?'

'At the moment, Mrs White, she's adamant that she wants a termination.'

'Well, she can put all that sort of nonsense right out of her head. Like I said, we've coped with this sort of thing before and we will again.'

'She seemed rather concerned about her father's reaction, Mrs White.'

'Oh, you leave him to me. I'll sort him out. I wasn't exactly lily-white when I came down the aisle.'

Mrs White left in a very different frame of mind from how she had arrived, after promising Frances she would return for a further appointment with Sarah after they'd had time to discuss things.

When she was alone again Frances thought deeply about whether or not she had handled things properly. Should she have told Mrs White the situation on the telephone, so preventing her several hours of worry? She sighed. Would she ever be sure that she had taken a correct course of action?

Alex hadn't returned to his room after Mrs White's departure, and as Frances knew she was the last patient of the afternoon she stood up and began tidying the desk, knowing that Alex always liked it left in an immaculate condition. Gathering up some loose forms she looked for a spare folder but, unable to find one, she opened the top drawer of the desk and slipped them inside. It was as she went to close the drawer that she remembered what June had told her.

Hesitating, she glanced up at the door but it remained tightly closed, then, with hands that shook slightly, she began to turn over several books and papers. It was near the bottom of the drawer, in a silver frame. A black and white photograph, it showed a young woman perhaps in her twenties with short dark hair cut into a fringe. Frances stared at it in disbelief—for apart from the eyes, which were dark, she could have been looking into a mirror.

CHAPTER NINE

THE days began to pass in a whirl of activity, and before she knew where she was Frances was into her third week at the surgery. By this time she had started to conduct her own surgeries, discussing the list afterwards with Alex, and she had even done a few house calls alone. She had also attended group days at the local hospital, where she had met up with the other trainees in the area. They had listened to lectures and swapped notes, comparing their respective surgery arrangements. Frances enjoyed these days but she was happiest when she was at the surgery.

She had also been attending tutorial evenings with Alex at Harbour Reach. At first she had been apprehensive about these, dubious about meeting his family again, but she needn't have worried because it seemed that Lucy spent every Wednesday evening at the home of her friend Emma, and Jeannie Cameron attended the local bridge club. Frances did, however, on the second of these evenings meet Alex's son, Nick.

He was a quiet, handsome boy with his father's dark eyes and classic profile. He shook hands gravely with her on being introduced, answered her brief questions about his chosen career, then politely excused himself and disappeared to his room.

Frances had found herself wondering if he had seen the resemblance to his mother, but if he had he gave no indication.

When she had found the photograph of Eloise and seen the likeness for herself it had strengthened her resolve not to allow any personal relationship between herself and Alex. But as the days passed and she found herself constantly in his company she realised it was becoming more and more difficult.

That there was a certain chemistry between them was undeniable and, the more she sought to pretend it didn't exist, the greater the tension was between them. She knew that Alex was as aware of it as she was, and because it found no outlet in rapport it was inevitable that at times nerves became frayed and tempers were aroused.

The third of her tutorials was on an evening when Alex had been absent from the surgery during the day at a lecture for trainers at the hospital and Frances had worked in conjunction with Neville. Kind as the senior partner was, Frances, in spite of all her good intentions, found she was longing for the evening when she would be with Alex again.

In the last couple of days she'd had a problem with Simon, who seemed to be under the illusion that because she went to lunch with him most days she should want to spend the rest of her spare time with him. In the end she'd had to be quite firm, making him understand that she wanted no long-term relationships. He'd gone off in a huff, leaving Frances upset because she hadn't wanted to hurt him.

By the time she arrived at Harbour Reach she felt tense and more apprehensive than usual. This wasn't helped by the fact that Alex's car wasn't in its usual place, and she realised he was still out.

She pressed the doorbell and while she waited turned and stared at the calm evening scene across the harbour. She was just thinking that there wasn't anyone at home when the door was opened and Lucy stood in the doorway, staring at her.

In one hand she held an open bottle of pink nail varnish, and glancing down Frances saw that she had painted the toenails on one foot.

'Oh, dear, I have called at a bad moment!' she said.

'Yes, you have rather, but you'd better come in.' The girl stood aside and Frances entered the house. 'Dad said you'd be coming. He rang about half an hour ago to say he'd been delayed and that he'd get home as soon as he could.'

'Are you alone?' asked Frances. She followed Lucy into the lounge, where the girl promptly sat down on the hearthrug and proceeded to paint the nails on her other foot.

'Yes; Nick's out with a friend and Jeannie's playing bridge. Emma's got a tummy upset, so you've got to put up with me.'

'Well, I'm jolly pleased about that, because I think it's high time we got to know one another,' said Frances pleasantly.

'Why?' Lucy looked up, the varnish brush poised in the air.

'Why what?'

'Why should it be time for us to get to know each other?'

Frances shrugged. 'I don't know. No particular reason. I just thought it would be nice, especially as I shall be working with your father for the next year.'

Lucy had the same suspicious expression on her face that Frances had seen when the girl had found her in the bathroom on that fateful Sunday morning, and suddenly she recalled Alex telling her that his daughter could be very possessive where he was concerned. She decided it was time she changed the subject to something safer. This child was far too perceptive, and Frances couldn't guarantee she wouldn't show any feelings if she were to discuss Alex too much.

'I hear you're interested in the theatre,' she said. 'I have a cousin on the West End stage.'

'Do you?' Immediately Frances knew she had gained Lucy's interest. The girl's dark eyes had grown enormous. 'How did she get there?'

'By years of hard work and dedication,' Frances replied, then added with a smile, 'And she's a he, by the way. James did a course in fine arts after completing his A Levels, then he attended stage school for three years before auditioning for a very small part in the chorus of a musical. It's been a long slog, but now at last his hard work's beginning to pay off.'

'That's what I keep telling Dad,' Lucy sighed, and absentmindedly pushed Mistoffelees away. He had

appeared from somewhere and was getting danger-
ously close to her wet nail varnish. 'But he's impossible,' she added with an exaggerated sigh. 'You just
wouldn't believe how archaic he is! He knows how
desperate I am to go to drama school, but do you
think he'll listen? I know I could get into a stage
school now, but he says I have to stay at school and
get some qualifications. I ask you, who needs boring
old qualifications these days!'

'He may have a point, you know, Lucy,' said
Frances, then as the girl would have interrupted she
carried on quickly, 'As I told you, James did his A
Levels then took an art diploma first.'

'But that will all take years,' wailed Lucy. 'I want
to do it now!'

'How old are you, Lucy?'

'Nearly sixteen. . .well, fifteen and a half.'

'And you're having tuition in drama and dance.'

She nodded enthusiastically.

'Well, I firmly believe that if you have true talent,
Lucy, it will come out, but maybe it would be better
if you were to continue as you are for the time
being. . .'

'Oh, you're as bad as Dad—we had a hell of a
row last night and I'm not sure that I'm even
speaking to him again yet. If he doesn't let me go,'
she tossed her burgundy hair back defiantly as she
replaced the cap on the nail varnish bottle, 'I shall
go off and join one of the dance troupes, like we
have on the pier in the summer show. Then he'll be
sorry,' she added darkly.

For a moment Frances was stuck for words. She

wasn't altogether sure that she had handled things very well by telling Lucy about her cousin, and now it sounded as if she might have encouraged her even further to defy her father. She looked up, then realised that the girl was staring at her curiously.

'What is it? Is there something wrong?'

'Jeannie said you looked like my mother,' she said bluntly, then as Frances floundered for something to say she added, 'But I don't think you do. My mother was small, she had brown eyes and yours are a funny greeny blue, and she grew her hair long and yours is short.'

At that moment Frances was relieved to hear Alex's car outside. Then, as he switched off the engine, slammed the door and inserted his key in the lock, Lucy rose gracefully to her feet and with her back as straight as a ramrod she disappeared up the spiral staircase.

Frances barely had time to recover before Alex appeared in the doorway, and his smile had her heart doing crazy things.

'Hello, sorry I'm late,' he said, then looking round the room he frowned. 'Hasn't Lucy been looking after you? I phoned and asked her——'

'Oh, yes,' Frances interrupted quickly, 'she has. She only just this minute went upstairs.'

He glanced up the stairs. 'Yes, I bet she did,' he said darkly. 'The temperature here got a bit high last night. Did she tell you?'

Frances looked uncomfortable, not wanting him to think she had been discussing him with his daughter. 'Well, she did say something,' she murmured.

He flung himself down on to the sofa and ran his hands through his hair. 'My God, it's not easy bringing up teenagers, you know.'

'No, I don't suppose it is,' she said quietly. 'And it can't help being on your own.'

She could have bitten out her tongue the moment she'd said it, but as she threw him a worried glance she was surprised to see that he didn't seem unduly perturbed. Instead he looked across at her and his expression softened.

'So how was your day? Has old Neville been driving you into the ground?'

'Not really. . . He's an old softie, isn't he?' She smiled. 'How did the trainers' day go?'

'Very predictably.' He yawned and passed a hand over his face, and for a moment Frances was struck by how tired he looked. He'd been on call the previous night and although he'd had several visits he hadn't called her out. He'd now had a long day, and what with his argument with Lucy she got the impression that it had all got the better of him.

'Have you eaten?' she asked, then added, 'Would you like me to get you something?'

'I had a meal at the hospital,' he replied. 'But a cup of tea would go down well.'

'OK.' With a laugh she got up and went through to the kitchen, where she soon found what she needed to make a pot of tea.

When she returned he had closed his eyes and was resting his head on the back of the sofa. Quietly she placed the tray on a small table and sat down beside him. He didn't stir, and she took the opportunity to watch him unobserved. His face was relaxed now, the lines of tension gone, and yet again Frances was struck by the perfect classic lines of his profile; the straight nose, dark brow and the firm jaw and slightly cleft chin below the full, well-shaped lips.

She felt a little thrill shoot through her as her gaze rested on his mouth. Had he really kissed her? Or had she imagined it? And if he had, had there really been so much fire and passion in it, or had that too been a figment of her imagination? Had it only been because of her resemblance to Eloise or had he felt something for her, Frances?

Just as she was despairing that she would ever know the answers, he suddenly opened his eyes. His surprised expression confirmed that he had slept for a few moments, then it was immediately replaced by a look of such longing as he gazed at her that her heart leapt. Their glances held and he reached out his hand and softly ran his fingers down her cheek. Fractionally she moved closer, holding her breath, anticipating his next move as little shivers fluttered down her spine.

'Frances. . . I. . .' He trailed off helplessly, then with a great sigh he shook his head and moved away from her.

The force of her frustration was almost physical, and to try to cover her confusion she attempted to pour the tea, but her hand shook and the spout of the teapot rattled against the cups.

'I think,' he said at last, breaking the almost unbearable silence, 'that it might be as well if we were to keep our tutorial short this evening.'

She nodded in reply, unable to trust her voice, then to her relief the phone rang and with a groan Alex hauled himself to his feet and crossed to the far side of the room to answer it. By the time he returned she had recovered her composure and had opened her briefcase and taken out her papers in an effort to appear professional.

For the next hour she had to force herself to concentrate as they discussed a new paper recently issued by the British Medical Association, then Alex turned the conversation to matters at the surgery, asking whom she had seen that day.

'I had a long consultation with Sarah White and her mother,' she replied thoughtfully.

'Sarah White?' He frowned, then glanced up with interest. 'Do you mean Bea's patient, the one who wanted termination?'

She nodded.

'And?'

'She's decided to have the baby.'

'Adoption?'

'Ah, that's still under discussion in the White household, but my opinion is that Mrs White would be horrified if her grandchild is "given up", as she puts it, and it's my guess that the child will be absorbed into the family.'

'Are you happy with that outcome?'

'That's not really the issue, is it? All I know is that for a time there Sarah White was my patient and she was miserable and confused; now she seems—not exactly happy but more positive, so yes, if you're asking if I'm satisfied with the way I handled the case, then I suppose I am.'

'Well done! I'm sure Bea will be suitably impressed. Anything else of note today?'

She hesitated, for she'd hoped he wouldn't ask that question, but now that he had she felt compelled to tell him of one case that had been bothering her all day. It had been a patient of his, a woman in her sixties whom she'd remembered coming to one of the very first of Alex's surgeries that she'd observed. He had previously been treating the woman for irritable bowel syndrome and had given her a repeat prescription and advice on her diet. That day, however, the woman had returned, complaining of altered bowel actions, and Frances had done a rectal examination.

'I had to refer her, Alex,' she told him.

'Why?' For a moment he looked surprised and slightly annoyed.

'Because I felt a mass high up in the rectum.'

He stared at her. 'I'm sure you're mistaken—I've watched that particular patient carefully and I'm certain that is not something I would have missed.'

She swallowed, but knew she had to stick to her guns. 'Well, I'm sorry, Alex, but I know what I felt.'

He continued to look annoyed, then he sighed and stood up. 'Well, for the patient's sake I hope you're wrong, but if you are right I'm glad you've spotted it now when there might be time to put it right. Now, I think it's time to call it a day. Did you bring your car?'

She shook her head, then stood up. 'No, it was such a lovely evening I walked over.'

'Right, in that case I'll walk back with you.'

'Oh, you don't need to. . .'

'Nonsense, the exercise will do me good.'

It was getting dark by the time they left Harbour Reach, the crimson glow behind the distant hills a perfect backdrop for the high mackerel sky.

'The tide's out,' said Alex, walking towards the harbour steps. 'Let's walk along the beach.'

Frances followed, only too aware of the tension that always seemed to exist between them, for if not on a personal basis, professional matters always provided another source of conflict.

They walked in silence over the firm wet sand and for the time being Frances was content to let the silence remain. Two men were digging for bait in the distance, but apart from them they were alone, the only sounds the calling of the gulls and the tinkling of a bell on a distant buoy. They walked close together, but not touching, and suddenly she was overcome with longing that he should put his arm around her or take her hand. He did neither, but the moment was one of such complete togetherness that he must have been aware of it.

Then as they turned the point of the harbour and the bay came into view with the lights from the promenade and the pier twinkling in the early dusk, the mood changed, and as if sensing it Alex broke the silence.

'I told you I'd be away at a seminar this weekend?'

'Yes, you did.' Her heart sank. 'But I've forgotten where you said it was being held.'

'London.' He replied briefly and she got the impression that he didn't particularly want to go. 'I should be on call on Saturday night. Simon has offered to cover, but I would like you to do it.'

She turned and stared at him in surprise.

'Don't you want to do it?' he asked abruptly.

'Of course I do,' she replied quickly. 'I didn't think you'd trust me, that's all. Especially with your being away.'

'I see no reason why you shouldn't, but I'll ask Simon to stand by in case you get something you can't handle. Are you happy with that?'

'Perfectly.' She hesitated. 'What about Lucy?'

'Lucy?' He frowned. 'What do you mean?' They had reached the rear of the surgery, and as he opened the gate in the wall he paused.

'I just wondered what she would be doing with you away.'

'Emma's mother has apparently asked her to spend the night with them.' He gave a short laugh. 'Besides, I doubt whether she'll even notice I've gone.'

A touch of bitterness had crept into his tone, and as they let themselves in the back door Frances said, 'Don't you think you're being rather hard on her, Alex?'

'What do you mean?' The frown on his forehead deepened and Frances knew she could be treading on dangerous ground, but she blundered on. There had been something about Lucy's attitude that evening that had bothered her.

'I think you should give her a chance and listen to her. She quite obviously loves the theatre and wants to make it her career, but she feels she's up against a brick wall where you're concerned.'

'Go on.' He raised his eyebrows and appeared to be listening intently, but there was a small, rather cynical smile playing around his lips, and Frances began to wish she'd kept her mouth shut.

'Well, don't you think you could compromise in some way?'

'And what do you suggest?' There was an icy note of sarcasm now in his tone, and her heart sank.

'I was thinking that if she agreed to stay on at school and finish her education perhaps you would see reason and at least discuss the possibility of her going to drama school when she's eighteen.'

He was silent for a moment as if reflecting on what she'd said, and she threw him a half-hopeful look. But her hopes were dashed barely a second later.

'Just because you've been dishing out advice in surgery to errant teenagers,' he said harshly, 'that doesn't make you an authority on all their problems.'

She caught her breath as his words stung like a slap, and she stared at him in dismay, then turning sharply she ran through the house and up the stairs.

He called after her once, but she took no notice, and reaching her flat she slammed the door then breathlessly leaned against it.

Tears were stinging the back of her eyes. How

dared he speak to her like that when she had only been trying to help? He might be her trainer, but that didn't give him the right to speak to her in that fashion.

Angrily she stormed into the bathroom stripping off her clothes as she went then, stepping into the shower, she lifted her face to the jet of water and after some moments felt at least some of her anger lift.

Afterwards she wrapped herself in a large fluffy towel and poured herself a drink. Normally she drank very little, but tonight she felt in dire need of something to relax her.

Tucking her feet under her, she curled up in the corner of her sofa and began flicking through the pages of a glossy magazine, but she found it impossible to concentrate as her thoughts constantly returned to Alex. In fact, she thought ruefully as she finally tossed the magazine aside, there were very few moments of the day now when he wasn't in her thoughts.

Until now she hadn't even wanted to consider the possibility that she was in love with him, but the more she tried to evade the issue the more it crept into her mind. But what would be the point even if she did admit it? The way things stood between them it would certainly be a very one-sided affair.

Restlessly she stood up, and pacing over to the mantelpiece she picked up one of her precious cats and moved its position. If only things were different! If only she bore no resemblance to Eloise, if only they didn't argue all the time. . .if only. . . Once

again she allowed her thoughts to wander, to fanta-
sise what it would be like to be possessed by Alex
Ryan.

So lost did she become in her impossible daydreams that she jumped violently as she suddenly
heard a door shut somewhere in the building. She
jerked her head up and listened. Then she smiled.
So he'd come back. Could it be that he was ashamed
at having spoken to her the way he had? Quickly she
discarded the towel that was still wrapped round
her, then she grabbed her bathrobe, slipped it on
and, securing it tightly, opened the door of her flat,
expecting to see Alex on the landing.

The place was in darkness, however, and there
was no further sound from downstairs. With a
puzzled frown Frances walked to the top of the stairs
and leaned over the banisters. She was about to call
out when she froze, for far below in the reception
hall she had caught sight of the beam from a torch.

For a moment she seemed incapable of moving,
then common sense returned and she knew she had
to get back into her flat and shut the door before the
intruder caught sight of the glow from her table lamp
and realised there was someone in the building.

Stealthily, inch by inch, she made her way back
across the landing, almost afraid to move as any
slight pressure made the floorboards creak. Once,
when she was nearly there, she heard a sound on the
first flight of stairs and her heart jumped in terror. If
the intruder was after drugs he could well be desperate and would stop at nothing.

At last, with a sob of relief, she got back inside.

Noiselessly she closed the door, slipped the bolt and switched off her light.

The room was plunged into darkness, then slowly, as her eyes became accustomed, she realised that moonlight was filtering through the blinds. Cautiously she edged her way across to the mantelpiece and with a shaking hand she reached out, fumbling under the edge until she found the panic button that Alex had had installed. With a little sob she pressed it. It was then that she heard the rattle of the doorhandle.

In sheer terror she stared at it then, crouching on the floor behind the door with her back against the wall, she put her arms over her head as the handle continued to be turned back and forth.

Oh, dear God, she prayed silently, please let the police come quickly!

The movement on the handle suddenly ceased and she heard the faint creak of a floorboard followed by silence, a mind-numbing silence that defied all measure of time.

Frances could not have said how long after it was that she heard loud footsteps on the stairs followed by the reassuring shout of the police. It could have been minutes or it could have been hours. She only really remembered finally opening the door and falling into Alex Ryan's arms.

CHAPTER TEN

ALEX had simply held Frances. Held her while the police took her statement, explaining that they had caught the intruder as he had attempted to escape through Neville's consulting-room window. Held her while he had explained that he was there because he had left instructions at the police station that if ever her panic alarm went off they were to inform him. And then he continued to hold her until she stopped shaking.

'Was it drugs they were after?' she asked.

'Probably—we won't know for sure until he's been questioned,' Alex replied, leading her to the settee where he sat down and drew her down beside him, still with one arm protectively around her.

'I don't think I've ever been so frightened in my life.' She shivered, and as he instinctively drew her closer she leaned against him. It seemed the most natural thing in the world for him to be there, to be comforting her when she needed him. He had obviously gone to bed and been awakened by the police, for he was more casually dressed than she had ever seen him, in denims, a sweatshirt, and trainers.

'I'm afraid,' he said after a while, 'that this will put you off staying on your own in this flat. I must admit I had my reservations when it was first suggested, it seemed so bleak and lonely up here.'

'But you did all you could to make it welcoming,' she said gently, and when he merely shrugged in response she added, 'No, Alex, I don't think this will make any difference, once I've had time to recover. I've become quite attached to my little retreat up here in the heavens—and, let's face it, the police have caught the culprit so he won't be coming back.'

They remained quiet for some time, then Frances all at once became aware that all she was wearing was her thin robe. She glanced down and saw that the belt had loosened and the front had fallen open, partly revealing the curve of her right breast.

Suddenly embarrassed, she pulled away from Alex and stood up. 'Would you like a drink?' She gave a nervous little laugh. 'I don't have any brandy, I'm afraid—but I should have something. . .'

'Shall I get it for you?'

'No. . .it's all right,' she replied quickly, needing to escape from his gaze. In the kitchen, out of his line of vision, she leaned against the sink, taking several deep breaths as she struggled to control herself. She still felt shaky, but whether this was from the shock she'd received or from the sudden intimacy in which she'd found herself with Alex, she didn't know.

She had turned and was reaching up to the cupboard for two glasses when she felt Alex's arms go round her. She hadn't heard him come into the kitchen behind her and she froze, her arms still above her head as for a moment he held her pressed closely against the taut hardness of his body.

Then as he lowered his head, burying his face in the vulnerable hollow between her neck and shoulder, she felt a knife-like edge of excitement shoot through her body, and it was in that instant that she knew without doubt that she loved him; loved him and wanted him with such intensity that it shook her to the very core. Nothing else mattered; the world outside ceased to exist as her senses heightened to the very peak of response. She closed her eyes, leaning her head against him and surrendering to the exquisite sensations, believing at that moment that nothing could excite her further. Then his hands began to mould the contours of her body beneath the thin substance of her wrap.

With a gasp of delight she gave herself up to the urgency of his mounting passion as he caressed her hips and thighs before drawing his hands up to cup her firm breasts, the nipples taut now and aching with desire.

With a groan he unfastened her belt, inched the silky fabric from her shoulders, then as the robe slid to her ankles he turned her to face him.

'Frances,' he whispered huskily, 'I want you.' Then, giving her no chance to speak or to protest, he gathered her up into his arms and carried her to the bedroom.

Moonlight flooded the room, and as Alex gently lowered her on to the bed and stretched out above her she entwined her arms around his neck, pulling his face down to hers. This time all the barriers that had been between them were down as they were now both powerless to resist the latent sexuality that had smouldered between them since they had first met and which had now flared into an inferno of desire.

Their lovemaking was everything she had ever dreamed it would be. Not simply a merging of their bodies—exciting as that in itself was—but a fusion of minds and their very souls. It was as if Alex took her on a journey, a journey of exploration and discovery that taught her things about her body and mind that she had never imagined, even in her wildest dreams.

And it hadn't ended there, for just when she thought there could surely be no more, when she lay satiated and exhausted in his arms, he aroused her again and again with hands and lips until her body cried out for sweet release and he would take her once more, raising her to even greater heights of ecstasy.

And all the while Alex, for his part, seemed delighted with her response to his experience and for the way she gave her love. So spontaneous was their lovemaking that Frances found it hard to believe that there had ever been any barriers between them.

Then for a time they slept but, as the first silvery fingers of dawn touched the sky, he reached out for her again and it was after that that the questions entered her mind. Lying together in a glorious tangle of sheets in the peaceful aftermath of their passion, she looked at Alex and saw a strange expression on his face.

'What is it, Alex?' she whispered, frightened now that the spell would be broken. 'What's wrong?'

He looked down at her and smiled, a rueful smile, then tenderly he traced his fingers down the side of her face. 'I was just wondering what we've done.'

She frowned. 'I know exactly what we've done, and I don't have any regrets.'

He didn't answer immediately, and she raised herself on to one elbow and looked down at him.

'Why?' she asked softly. 'Do you?'

He sighed. 'If only it were that easy.'

'Why can't it be?'

'There are many reasons, Frances, but this is sheer madness, you know.'

She bit her lip, her happiness rapidly evaporating, then suddenly she had to know. 'Is it because I look like Eloise?' she asked breathlessly.

He stared at her. 'Who told you that?'

'Jeannie Cameron.'

'What in the world made her say that?'

'It was that first time I met her—I was sitting in the kitchen alone and she came in unexpectedly. I startled her, and she said that for a moment she had thought I was Eloise.' She glanced at him to see his reaction, but he was staring at the window where the sky was now lightening rapidly. She wondered what he was thinking. 'But Lucy and Nick don't seem to have noticed anything,' she added. 'In fact, Lucy told me that Jeannie had mentioned it to her, but I don't think she agreed.'

'I'm afraid Lucy has rather different memories of the way her mother looked,' he replied grimly.

'Jeannie said I looked the way Eloise did when she first met you.'

'You must remember Eloise was a relative of Jeannie's and Jeannie watched her grow up. She knew her very well.'

'And did you see the resemblance?' She held her breath as she waited for his reply, agonising that he would put into words what she had feared all along.

At last he turned his head and his eyes met hers. 'Of course I did. I didn't realise it at first when I met you at the hospital, but then when you arrived at the surgery you'd changed your hairstyle, and the difference was unbelievable. You looked the image of how I remembered Eloise when we had first met.'

'And it bothered you.' She said it flatly, and it was a statement rather than a question.

'Yes,' he admitted. 'It bothered me.'

'Is that why you were so aloof with me?'

He smiled, and the look of tenderness that came into his eyes almost melted her bones. 'Was I?' He shrugged. 'Yes, I suppose I was a bit of a pig. But I had to be, Frances. The only way I felt I could handle the situation was to keep you at arm's length.'

'And now. . .?' she breathed.

'Now?'

'Is that all this means to you? The fact that I remind you so intensely of your late wife?' A note of anguish had crept into her voice, and he was quick to pick it up.

Reaching forward he pulled her against him, cradling her head against the dark hair on his chest. 'Of course not!' He said it fiercely, his grip tightening, and for a moment she felt a spark of hope. 'Frances, you must believe me, that was only the way I felt at the beginning. Now, after getting to know you, working with you, and now this. . .what I feel is for you, and you alone, not for an echo from the past. You are you, Frances, and you are totally different from Eloise.'

'Then why did you say that what we've done is madness?' She lifted her head from his chest and tried to look again into his eyes, but he sighed and avoided her stare. When he didn't reply, she asked quietly, 'Is it Sandra?'

'Sandra?' He looked down at her blankly.

'Yes, Sandra—Sandra Jones.'

'What does she have to do with anything?'

'I just thought that maybe she and you. . .' She trailed off as she saw his incredulous expression.

'Good lord, no. Sandra Jones isn't my type at all.'

'In that case I think perhaps you'd better make that fact plain to her,' said Frances firmly. 'Because, believe me, she's under the impression that things are about to happen between you, and she isn't the only one.'

He stared at her. 'What are you talking about?'

'I would lay odds that half the staff are waiting for something to happen as well.'

He groaned and leaned back against the headboard. 'Why is it if you show a little kindness to someone it's immediately misconstrued? I felt rather sorry for Sandra after her husband left her and I took her to lunch a few times, but that's all. I did at one time suspect Sybil of matchmaking, but I had no idea it had reached such proportions. Besides, she's my patient.'

'Not any more,' Frances replied drily. 'Apparently she's changed doctors.'

'I think you know a darn sight more about what's going on within the practice than I do, and I've been here five years and you've been here—how long? A month?'

Frances was staring at him, and while she was listening to what he was saying her mind was racing ahead, and when he stopped she nodded, then said, 'Alex, just now you called it madness, what had happened, but I don't understand. If it isn't because I bring back painful memories of Eloise, and it isn't because you're having a relationship with Sandra, then what is wrong?'

For a moment he closed his eyes as if he was fighting some inner battle, then looking at her again he said, 'It's because of you, my love.'

Her spine tingled at the endearment. 'Me. . . But. . .?'

He took a deep breath. 'Frances, listen to me, please. This can never work between us; for a start, I'm far too old for you; secondly, I have a family and it just wouldn't be fair to land you with a couple of teenagers, especially a stroppy one like Lucy— and if that isn't enough, I am your trainer.'

'Oh, is that all?' Frances laughed, unable to

disguise the sudden rush of happiness that threatened to overwhelm her. 'I thought you were going to say something serious!'

'But, Frances, it is serious.'

'What is?' she demanded. 'The fact that you're my trainer? It isn't illegal, is it? Are you likely to be struck off?'

'Well, no, I don't think so. To tell you the truth, I can't ever remember hearing of a trainee having an affair with a trainer before. . . I honestly don't know, it could be frowned upon, and I couldn't let anything jeopardise your career.'

'It won't, Alex—it won't, I promise you.' Suddenly she felt elated, because as far as she was concerned the obstacles he had put forward were nothing compared to the ones she had feared. She hadn't been able to cope with the possibility that he might have only found her attractive because of reminders of Eloise; neither could she have coped with it if he'd said he had been in love with Sandra. Now, as it was. . . Impulsively, she turned to him, running her hands over his chest and across his shoulders, instinctively drawing him closer.

'But that's the least of the worries. . . Frances, there's too big an age difference between us.'

'Rubbish—I've always preferred older men. I think I've probably got a father fixation.'

He groaned. 'Don't. . .please. Anyway, I'm not that much older!'

'Well, then, stop worrying about it. I always did find younger men immature.'

'What about your doctor friend, from medical school?'

She grimaced. 'Especially him.' Alex raised his eyebrows and she continued, 'It was fun while it lasted, but it's over now, Alex, between Andrew and me.'

'And Simon?'

'That never even started, I can assure you.'

He smiled then and she snuggled closer to him. 'You might as well give in, you know—the problems are all in your mind.'

'Not quite. There's still Nick. . .and Lucy.'

'Ah, Nick is a love, and Lucy—well, Lucy is just a mixed-up little girl who needs lots of love and a little understanding. In fact, nothing I can't handle.'

'Don't underestimate my daughter,' he replied darkly.

'I don't intend to.'

He was silent, obviously reflecting on what they had said, then with a sigh he turned to her clock on the bedside cabinet. 'If we're to avert a full-scale scandal I really should be thinking of moving,' he said.

But Frances caught the note of reluctance in his voice and pressed herself against him again, and he, with a groan of defeat, reached out for her once more, taking her again swiftly and expertly, only finally leaving her when she lay utterly fulfilled and at peace.

He had eventually gone back to Harbour Reach to shower and change for surgery, and Frances had herself showered and dressed before making some toast and coffee.

In spite of the difficulties Alex had put forward she felt confident and happy. She had no qualms about the difference in their ages and had hardly thought about it until he had mentioned it; neither was she concerned about the fact that he was her trainer. She did, however, recognise that they might have to face problems with his family, and she was not naïve enough to believe that Lucy would exactly welcome her with open arms. In spite of this she remained optimistic, for the night she had just spent with Alex had proved beyond doubt that he was the only man for her.

When he had left, it had been with a promise that they would discuss things more fully after his return from the weekend seminar in London.

Frances wasn't sure how she got through the following two days. They seemed to pass in a rosy haze, and although she and Alex agreed not to say anything for the time being at the surgery it soon became evident that their relationship had changed. This was accepted in different ways by the other members of staff. June was one of the first to detect a change, and over coffee she casually made reference to the fact. Frances skilfully avoided a direct reply, but later she became aware of other subtleties, such as giggling among the reception staff, open hostility from Sandra, and, on the day before Alex went to London, confrontation from Simon.

It was over lunch at the pub, after they had

discussd his standing by over the weekend in case Frances required assistance, that he brought up the subject of the break-in.

'I imagine you'll now be on the look-out for somewhere else to live,' he said as Mandy brought their lunch to their table.

'Why?' Frances sipped her drink and carefully set it down, sensing what was to come.

'Well, you can hardly be wanting to stay in that flat.'

'I don't see why not. I like it there. I've made it home.'

'Yes, but aren't you nervous up there alone?'

She hesitated. 'Not really, Simon. Alex asked me the same question and, as I explained to him, they've caught the guy who broke in, so he's not likely to come back. It might have been a different matter if he was still at large.'

'Yes, but it could happen again. . .'

'Hey, come off it, Simon, what are you trying to do? Unnerve me completely?' She laughed as she bit into her salad roll.

'Yes,' he said calmly. 'Something like that, because I've heard that one of the apartments where I live is coming empty and I thought it would suit you down to the ground.'

'Oh, I don't think so. . .' Frances began, but Simon leaned forward and put his hand over hers.

'Don't decide yet, Frances. Think about it, please. It could be great, you know. We could have fun, you and I.'

She glanced up, her eyes met his and she knew

exactly from the expression in his just what sort of fun he meant. She took a deep breath. She knew she had to put him straight once and for all. 'Simon, I'm sorry, but I don't need any time to think about it. I'm quite happy in my little flat, and you and I won't be having the sort of fun you're thinking of.' She looked him straight in the eye as she spoke, and for a moment she was taken aback as she saw the brief expression of pain that crossed his features. In that instant it dawned on her that Simon wasn't only just out for a bit of fun, but that he had become genuinely fond of her. She bit her lip and knew that, now more than ever, she must leave him under no illusions.

'I am sorry,' she repeated.

He didn't answer immediately, then quietly he said, 'It's Alex, isn't it, Frances?'

She hesitated, uncertain at this precarious stage how much she should say, then she nodded. 'Yes,' she said, and her voice was little more than a whisper so that he had to lean forward to hear.

He sighed. 'Well, I hope you know what you're doing. But I'd hate you to get hurt, Frances. You aren't the first to be smitten by the Ryan charm and I doubt whether you'll be the last.'

She gave a slight shrug. 'It's a chance I'm prepared to take, Simon,' she said, then glancing at her watch she reminded him it was time they were getting back to the surgery.

CHAPTER ELEVEN

IT HAD been arranged for Frances to take the Saturday morning surgery with Simon. He was to see the local patients and she would take the temporary residents. It turned out to be a fairly quiet morning, as was so often the case on a Saturday in a seaside resort. It was change-over day, and many visitors were on their way home and the new intake hadn't yet arrived. Frances took advantage of the situation by catching up on a mountain of paperwork.

It was as she was working steadily through the morning mail that she came across a letter from a consultant at the local hospital confirming the presence of a rectal mass in the woman who had come to see her. She stared thoughtfully at the letter, wondering what Alex's reaction would be when he saw that the patient was to be admitted immediately for further investigation and possible surgery. She knew he would ultimately be pleased if it was found that they had acted in time, but, human nature being what it was, she also wondered how he would feel about the fact that she had discovered what he had missed. She decided that probably the best way to handle it would be to discreetly avoid mentioning it to him. As her thoughts automatically turned to him, something that was happening with increasing frequency with every passing day, she sighed, and setting down her pen she stood up and walked to the window.

There was a decided change in the climate that day and it had reverted to the rough squally weather that had greeted her arrival a month ago. The sea was grey, the waves white-capped and angry while the gulls screeched and swooped overhead in their never-ending search for food. Alex had left for London very early that morning and he had come up to the flat late the night before to say goodbye.

Her heart skipped a beat as she recalled their passionate lovemaking, which had somehow ended in an argument about the way she had treated one of his patients. She sighed again and turned from the window. If their relationship did continue, and she wanted that more than anything else in the world, then she knew it would almost certainly be a stormy one. They were two strong-minded, passionate individuals with very clear-cut opinions. He had, however, before leaving, confirmed his promise that on his return they would talk and try to resolve some of their difficulties.

To Frances none of the problems he had put forward was insurmountable, but she knew that Alex still had grave reservations, especially about their age difference and the fact that he had a family. But he could not hide the way he felt about her, and as far as Frances was concerned that was all she needed—the rest was superfluous.

She was jolted from her daydreams by the sudden

arrival of Beverley, who informed her that a child had just been brought in having trapped its fingers in a car door. Frances made her way to the treatment-room to the accompaniment of the child's terrified screams.

This accident seemed to trigger off an influx of patients, and for the rest of the morning Frances was kept busy with no more time to indulge in any fond thoughts of Alex.

At the end of the morning she met up with Simon in Reception. Beverley was just leaving, and as Frances let her out of the front door she said, 'Hope the weekend isn't too hectic for you, Frances.'

Frances pulled a face and dropping the catch on the door turned to face Simon.

'Now, don't forget,' he said briskly, picking up his case, 'I'll be at home if you need anything. You have my number?'

She nodded. 'Yes, but——'

'Well, I'll leave you to it, then.' With a curt nod he opened the door and stepped outside, and moments later Frances heard the roar of his sports car. With a sigh she again locked the door then, turning, leaned against it for a moment. She suddenly felt very much alone and very responsible for the residents of Pebblecoombe. She had been about to suggest lunch to Simon, either upstairs in her flat or by taking a bleeper with them to the pub in case ambulance control needed to contact her. But since her recent talk with him he had been very cool towards her, and she bitterly regretted it—not the fact that she had put him in the picture regarding

Alex and herself, but because she didn't want to lose his friendship. She also hadn't wanted to hurt him, for he had been kind to her since her arrival and had obviously become very fond of her.

Wearily she made her way upstairs to her flat, where she prepared a light lunch for herself. Her feeling of loneliness intensified, and she realised she was desperately missing Alex.

It was almost a relief when the phone rang and she took a call from a social worker involved with Mr Buckley, the elderly man she had visited with Alex when she had first arrived at the surgery. The old man was having difficulties with his breathing again, and Frances said she would go over right away. She immediately dialled ambulance control to tell them she was reverting to her bleeper, then picking up her case she hurried downstairs and outside to her car.

When she arrived at the flats the social worker let her in, and she found Mr Buckley to be in a great deal of distress. After examining him she diagnosed bronchial pneumonia and, after consultation with the social worker about responsibility for his care, she phoned the hospital and asked to speak to the medical registrar.

She carefully explained, but he hedged, saying he was short of beds and that he would have to check the situation. While Frances waited for his decision she found herself remembering how it had been when she had been a houseman and had to placate a demanding GP. Now she was in the role of GP and the picture seemed very different. At last the arrangements were made, the hospital agreed to take Mr Buckley, and Frances sat with him until the ambulance arrived.

As she watched his laboured breathing she wondered if Alex would have agreed with her decision or whether he would have still insisted on the old man remaining in his own home. She had no way of knowing, however, and could only trust her own judgement.

The doors of the ambulance had barely closed before her bleeper sounded and Frances was off on another call. This was to set the pace for the rest of the day, with one emergency following another, leaving her little time to reflect on what she was doing or her own problems. She had already decided she would only call on Simon in a dire emergency.

During the evening she was returning from a call to one of the hotels where a temporary resident had suffered an angina attack after the shock of discovering that he had come on holiday and left all his medication at home, when on a sudden impulse she decided to call in at Harbour Reach and see if Lucy was still at home.

She knew that Alex had said that his daughter would be spending the night with her friend Emma, but she thought there might be a chance that she hadn't yet left.

The house, however, was silent and there was no reply when she rang the doorbell. As she walked away she was again overcome by an unexpected surge of loneliness, and this time she knew it was because Alex was away.

It was as she was driving home along the promenade that she suddenly saw Lucy. She was with a crowd of young people sitting on the sea wall, and as Frances approached she glanced up.

Frances waved and smiled, but Lucy looked the other way, pretending not to have seen her. With a grimace she continued on to the surgery, reluctantly admitting to herself that Alex could be right and that she would have a battle on her hands with a certain young lady when she found out about her relationship with her father.

It was very late when Alex phoned, and Frances was in bed.

'Did I wake you?' he asked.

'No, I was hoping you would phone,' she replied, suddenly swamped with feelings of longing for him and wishing he was beside her in bed.

'How has your day been?'

'Oh, not bad. Not bad at all,' she lied, determined she wasn't going to risk an argument by mentioning specific cases. 'How about you?'

'Rather boring, actually,' he said.

'Really? I thought you said you were looking forward to the lecture this evening, that it was a speaker you particularly wanted to hear?'

'It was.' He paused. 'But I couldn't concentrate.'

'And why was that?' She held her breath.

'Because there's this girl I can't get out of my mind.'

'Oh? Anyone I know? What's she like?'

'She's fabulous. She has the most gorgeous dark hair, strange eyes that are neither green nor blue, and she haunts me every moment of the day and night. Do you have a remedy for that, Dr Marriott?'

'It sounds to me like a severe case of unrequited passion,' she said with a low chuckle. 'And as far as I know, the only treatment is constant attention.'

'Well, Doctor, I'm sure you know best, so I'll be home as soon as I can.'

'See you soon, Alex,' she whispered.

'Goodnight. Oh, and Frances?'

'Yes?'

'I love you.'

The line went dead and for several moments she stared at it, then, hugging her pillow, she at last fell into an exhausted sleep.

She was awoken by the persistent ringing of the telephone and struggling from the depths of sleep she groped for the receiver.

'Hello?' she mumbled.

'Dr Marriott? It's Pebblecoombe Police. Sergeant Hawkins.'

'Oh. . .oh, yes, Sergeant.' Frances immediately recognised the deep southern accent of the policeman who had come to the surgery on the night of the break-in. Frantically she fumbled for the light switch, then glancing at the clock she saw it was ten past one. 'What can I do for you?'

'I was told you're on call, is that correct?'

'Yes, Sergeant, unfortunately it is.'

'Well, Doctor, we've had a call from the coast-guard. Apparently there's been an incident on the beach to the west of the pier below the cliffs. They are requesting the attendance of a doctor.'

'Right.' Already Frances was struggling out of bed. 'Do we know the nature of the incident?'

'Two people were reported in difficulties in the water, so it may be a possible drowning. We don't know for sure.'

'I'll be there in a few minutes.'

By this time Frances was wide awake and, flinging on a tracksuit and trainers, she grabbed an anorak and her case.

As she stepped from the front door she was greeted by a roaring sound and for a moment she was puzzled, then she realised it was the sound of the sea. The wind had risen again blowing ragged clouds across a wild sky, and, as Frances drove along the promenade, in the intermittent bursts of moonlight she caught glimpses of ribbons of foaming white surf as it crashed on to the beach. She shivered slightly, wondering what anyone could be doing in the sea on a night like this, then thinking that it must be that a boat had capsized.

She had no difficulty in finding the location at the base of the cliffs, for even from a distance she could see the blue flashing lights of several police cars, and as she stopped and scrambled from her car she saw the coastguard's Land Rover was among them as well.

A police officer met her and escorted her across the beach to a small cove where the glow from a huge barbecue illuminated the scene. As they approached he gave her a rapid update of the situation.

'We believe it's a wild party that got out of hand—there's evidence of large quantities of alcohol and possibly drugs—cannabis, we think. Some horseplay followed, with several individuals going fully clothed into the sea, we think for a dare. Two persons have been reported missing. Ah, it looks as if the coast-guards are bringing someone in now.'

There seemed to Frances to be dozens of young people on the beach, their faces ashen, tinged with blue from the lights of the vehicles as they watched, clustered in silent little groups as the first person was carried from the sea.

Frances saw that he was a young man in his early twenties. His hair was plastered to his face, his eyes were closed and he was wearing tattered jeans and a sweatshirt.

She instructed the coastguards to lay him down, then with a feeling of dread in her heart she felt for a pulse, then attempted to resuscitate him using cardiac massage. She knew it was hopeless even as she began, but still she went on. The only sound from the group of watchers was of a girl sobbing. Then a shout went up from further along the beach, and, looking up, Frances saw that the guards had retrieved a second figure from the sea and were beckoning to her.

It was as she stood up and indicated for the police officer to cover the still figure on the sand that she suddenly saw the white, shocked face of a young girl on the edge of the crowd. With a jolt she realised it was Lucy, and for a brief moment their eyes met, then Frances hurried off to the second victim of that night's madness.

This time, however, there was hope, for she detected a faint pulse in the boy's neck, and immediately she set to work pumping the water from his lungs before clearing his airways and administering mouth-to-mouth resuscitation.

She worked untiringly, and her reward finally came when he choked and spluttered and began breathing normally. By this time an ambulance had arrived, and Frances stood back and watched as the boy was lifted on to a stretcher and carried away. The police were gathering the youngsters together for questioning, but when Frances looked round for Lucy she couldn't see her.

'Thank you, Dr Marriott, you've done a fine job.' It was the police officer speaking, and reluctantly Frances abandoned her search for Lucy. There would have been little she could have done anyway, but somehow she felt responsible for her, especially with Alex away. God only knew what he would say when he found out that his daughter had been at a party like that when he had been under the impression that she had been safe at Emma's home.

'What about the rest of these youngsters?' she asked the policeman.

He shrugged. 'Some will be taken to the station for questioning. The rest will be sent home.' Turning away from the still silent, shocked crowd, he escorted Frances back to her car.

* * *

She slept fitfully for the rest of the night, haunted by two faces; one Lucy's, shocked and white, and the other of the boy who had drowned so needlessly. Then at dawn she was called out to a middle-aged man, a patient of Neville's who had passed a kidney stone and was in severe pain.

At about ten o'clock her phone rang again. This time it was Lucy.

'Is Dr Mitchell on call, Frances?' she asked in a very small voice.

'No, it's just me this weekend, Lucy.'

'Oh. . .well. . .thank you.'

It sounded as if she was about to hang up, so Frances intervened swiftly. 'What is it, Lucy? Why did you want Dr Mitchell?'

'It's Emma, she's registered with Dr Mitchell and she keeps being sick. . .'

'Where are you?'

'At Emma's house.'

'Isn't her mother there?'

There was a moment's silence, then Lucy said, 'No, her parents are away for the weekend.'

'Away? But I thought. . .oh, never mind. I'll be right over—give me Emma's address.'

She scribbled down the address, tore it off her pad and hung up, then drained her coffee-mug and hurried downstairs.

In the car park she met Simon.

'Hello, Frances. Is everything all right?' He looked concerned.

'Yes, why?'

'Well, I just heard about last night. Why didn't you call me?'

She shrugged. 'I didn't see any need. You couldn't have done any more than I did; the other lad was dead when he was brought out of the sea.'

'Oh, I'm not suggesting. . .it's just that you seem to be having a hectic time. Is there anything I can do for you now?' He glanced down at her case as he spoke.

'No, it's OK, thanks, I'm fine,' she replied.

'Well, all right, then, if you're sure.' He looked a bit uncomfortable, as if he regretted being offhand with her the previous day. 'But you will give me a ring, if you want help, won't you?'

'Of course I will.' She smiled and noticed that he looked relieved. There was no way he would want Alex thinking that he'd left her to cope with more than she could handle.

'I'll see you later, then.' He turned to get into his car, then paused. 'Oh, Frances, by the way, the police were most impressed with the way you coped last night.'

She drove to Emma's feeling almost light-hearted but after one look at Lucy's expression, which was a mixture of guilt and fear, she felt her spirits plummet.

Emma was in bed and seemed to be suffering from a combination of shock and the effects of too much vodka. After Frances had treated her and given her some medication from her case to ease the nausea, she went downstairs to where Lucy was waiting apprehensively in the hall.

'Will she be all right?' she asked, glancing up the stairs as she spoke.

Frances nodded. 'Yes, leave her to rest and she'll be fine. But what about you?' She stared keenly at the young girl, who was still very white with violet shadows beneath her eyes, which looked enormous in her tiny face. 'Have you slept at all?'

She shook her head. 'I couldn't. . . I kept seeing. . .seeing. . .' Her lip trembled and her eyes glistened with sudden tears.

Firmly Frances guided her into the lounge and indicated for her to sit down on a sofa.

'Did you know those two boys very well? Were they friends?' she asked quietly.

Lucy shook her head. 'No, not really. I knew them by sight, but it was some of the others who asked us to the party. I wish now we'd never gone.'

'Where did Emma's parents think you spent the night?'

'At my house. . .' She looked down at the carpet, then suddenly she looked up again. 'I suppose you'll tell my dad?'

'What makes you think I'll do that?'

'Well, you're pretty good friends, aren't you?'

'Yes, we are,' she admitted. 'But that doesn't give me the right to betray your confidence.'

'You mean you won't tell him?' Lucy stared at her in amazement.

Frances shook her head. 'He won't hear about it from me, I promise—but Lucy, you must remember, this is a small town, news travels fast, and he could well hear about it from another source.'

'Well, that's a chance I'll have to take.'

'What about the police? Didn't they question you at the station? I would have thought there was a very good chance they might be getting in touch with a few parents, if what I saw was anything to go by.'

Lucy looked down again. 'We didn't have to go to the station. They asked us some questions on the beach, then they said we could go home, but they did say they may want to speak to us again,' she admitted gloomily.

'They mentioned something about drugs. Do you know anything about that, Lucy?' asked Frances sharply.

Something in the tone of her voice made Lucy jerk her head up, then looking Frances straight in the eye she said, 'No, Frances, I swear to you if there were drugs there, we didn't know. I would never get into that scene. . .you must believe me!'

Frances nodded. 'I'm glad to hear it, but what about the drink? Vodka, wasn't it, from what Emma told me?'

Lucy hung her head again. 'But everyone drinks. . .absolutely everyone. . .'

'You're under age, Lucy,' said Frances firmly. 'Don't you think you're letting your father down by your behaviour?'

'He doesn't care what I do,' Lucy retorted.

Frances stared at her, fighting the sudden urge to shake her. 'Well, that's just where you're wrong, young lady! Your father thinks the world of you——'

'Hah! That's what you think. If he did, he'd let

me go to drama school,' she retorted, then fell silent as her eyes filled up again. Helplessly she stared at Frances, then, taking the handkerchief she offered, she blew her nose fiercely. 'It was awful last night— I just wish I could stop thinking about it, but I can't. I keep seeing that boy, the one who drowned. Only a few minutes before, he was eating sausages from the barbecue and laughing. . . He. . .' She gave a great gulp that ended in a sob.

Frances sat quietly, waiting for her to get herself under control again, then she said, 'Lucy, you've been playing at being grown up, haven't you? Well, if you do that I'm afraid you have to take the responsibilities that go with it. Last night you and Emma learnt a very harsh lesson, but let's hope it's one that won't have to be repeated.'

As last she stood up and, looking down at the pathetic little figure huddled on the sofa, she said, 'I must get back to the surgery now, Lucy. Will you be all right?'

She nodded. 'Yes, I'll be OK. I'll stay until I'm sure Emma's all right, then I'll get home.'

Frances frowned. 'Your dad won't be home until tomorrow—will Jeannie be there?'

Lucy nodded, then shuddered. 'I hope she doesn't get to hear about last night. She'd kill me if she knew I'd lied to her.'

As Frances drove back to the surgery she found herself wondering just what Alex's reaction would be if he found out. As she had promised Lucy, her father wouldn't hear about his daughter's involvement from her, but there was no guarantee that he wouldn't hear from someone else.

She carried on taking calls until late afternoon when Simon arrived and insisted on taking over from her for the night. She wasn't really sorry to hand over the bleeper and to know that because she wasn't likely to be called out she would be there if Alex called again during the evening.

It was about nine o'clock when, waiting as she had been for the telephone to ring, she was startled by a knock on her door. Since the break-in she took no chances and called through the door, asking the identity of her visitor.

The reply, deep and slightly husky, caused her heart to leap uncontrollably, and flinging open the door she gave a little cry of delight to see Alex leaning against the doorframe.

CHAPTER TWELVE

'ALEX! Whatever are you doing here? I didn't think you were coming home until tomorrow.'

His smile had a sheepish, almost schoolboy quality about it as Frances stepped aside to let him in.

'Neither did I,' he admitted, then added, 'but I couldn't stand it any longer.'

'Oh, dear, was it that bad? Was it the lectures or the accommodation?' she asked innocently as he strode past her and began prowling around her flat, peering at her ornaments.

He didn't answer immediately, then, turning from the mantelpiece, he looked into her eyes and her heart skipped a beat.

'Nothing like that,' he replied shortly, then in a couple of strides he was across the room and enfolding her in his arms. 'I just couldn't bear to be away from you a moment longer.' Hungrily his mouth searched for hers, possessing her lips in a kiss of equal measures of passion and tenderness.

Breathlessly she leaned against him, her senses spinning as it briefly registered in her brain that now not only had he told her he loved her, but he had also admitted he needed her to such an extent that he couldn't bear to be without her. Winding her arms around his neck, she threw back her head, and gave a small laugh of pure joy just as he lowered his head to her breasts.

Their lovemaking was every bit as tumultuous and full of fire as before, and this time when it was over and she lay quietly in his arms Frances knew without a shadow of doubt that she had found the man she wanted beside her for the rest of her life.

It wasn't until much later, as he idly traced patterns across her bare shoulders, that he asked about her weekend, and with a pang she was jolted back to reality.

'Anything exciting happen?' he asked casually.

She hesitated, not wanting to spoil the magic of the moment but knowing that she had to say something. 'I was called to an accident on the beach last night.'

'On the beach?' He frowned.

'Yes. One boy was drowned, but I was able to resuscitate another.'

He stared at her. 'Whatever happened?'

She took a deep breath. 'They were at a party— some barbecue. . . I think it got a bit out of hand and some of them ended up in the water for a dare, but apparently the tide turned, the sea was terribly rough anyway, and the two of them got carried out. The police called me,' she added as an afterthought, desperately hoping he wouldn't ask any more questions.

'I suppose it was the usual gang,' he said grimly, linking his hands behind his head.

'What do you mean?' She hardly dared to look at him.

'Well, Sergeant Hawkins was telling me only a few weeks ago that they've been keeping an eye on a gang of local kids, all from well-off families, incidentally, who've been holding these wild parties at weekends. Apparently there's been evidence of drugs being used, and I know the police were particularly keen to stamp the whole thing out.'

Frances swallowed and, not trusting herself to speak, merely nodded in reply.

'So you were in on some action the minute my back was turned.'

She threw him an apprehensive glance, but was relieved to see a glimmer of admiration in his eyes. 'Did Simon give you a hand?' he asked.

She shook her head and his eyes narrowed. 'Oh, he did offer,' she added hastily, 'but I wanted to see if I could cope alone.'

'Has he taken over now?'

'Yes.'

'Good, so we won't be disturbed.' He reached out for her again, then paused. 'Oh, I have a present for you,' he said casually, and leaning over the side of the bed he lifted his brown leather jacket up from the floor where he had tossed it earlier in his haste. He rummaged in the pockets while Frances watched in growing anticipation, then he pulled out a small round box shaped like a hatbox and handed it to her. 'Open it,' he instructed, adding, 'I saw it in a shop window in the Burlington Arcade.'

Cautiously she lifted the lid and removed a wodge of tissue paper before peering into the box, then with a cry of delight she lifted out a miniature black cat. It had a decided Oriental look about it, and Frances placed it in the palm of her hand to admire it.

'It's beautiful, Alex,' she breathed. 'Quite exquisite.'

'It's made of black jade,' he explained. 'And when the man in the shop told me the meaning of black jade I knew it was meant for you.'

She looked up, puzzled. 'What do you mean?'

'You know how you've constantly assured me you like it up here in your flat in the heavens?'

She nodded, completely mystified now.

'Well, apparently in China, where this little fellow came from, black jade is known as the Jewel of Heaven.'

He had stayed with her until late, only leaving when he did because he feared there would be speculation the following morning among the staff. She was deeply touched by his apparent concern for her reputation, just as she was touched and delighted by the unexpected romantic side to his nature which had been revealed in so many little ways.

She awoke the following morning in an optimistic frame of mind, convinced now that the growing strength of their love would overcome any problems. With a little secret smile she placed the tiny Chinese cat in pride of place on her shelf before going down to face a Monday morning surgery.

It proved to be extremely busy, as she had anticipated, and there was time for little more than a brief secret glance between herself and Alex, but it was enough; enough to know he was thinking of her.

At lunchtime, Simon once again asked her to go to the pub with him and, while she had been looking forward to a brief time with Alex, at the same time she wanted to get things back on to a friendly, even keel with Simon. She stole a quick moment to explain to Alex, and he smiled, telling her not to worry as he was meeting Nick in town to help him buy reference books for the new school term.

She enjoyed her lunch, for Simon was back to his old self, having apparently accepted her feelings for Alex and decided philosophically there was nothing he could do about them. She was still in the same happy frame of mind when she returned to the surgery to assist with an antenatal clinic.

The first patient was Sarah White, and Frances was pleased to find that the girl's attitude to the coming baby seemed to have changed drastically since she had learned of her mother's reaction. After the usual routine procedures of examination, checking weight, urine and blood-pressure, Frances had a chat with the girl.

She seemed less rebellious now and almost as if she had accepted that apart from adoption there was another option in that with help from her parents she could keep the child.

'Well, it's like I said before,' said Sarah as she stood up to go, 'I don't see why I should cart it around all that time just to give it away.'

Frances smiled as she watched the girl flick back her straggly hair and leave the room.

The smile was still on her face when the door was almost immediately flung open again and Alex stood there.

'Why, Alex. . .' The greeting died on her lips at the same instant as her smile disappeared, for far from this being some stolen moment of bliss, which was what she had at first hoped it might be, the expression on his face was one of barely controlled fury.

'What the hell has been going on?' he demanded, kicking the door shut behind him.

She swallowed, instinct telling her what was wrong. 'What do you mean?' she asked, playing for time.

'What do I mean? I think you know very well what I mean, Frances!' She remained silent, and he stared at her as if there was something about her he was finding difficult to understand, then he said, 'Why couldn't you have seen fit to tell me that my daughter was at that party?'

She took a deep breath. 'I didn't see that it was my place to do so.'

'What?' He stared at her incredulously, and in spite of the tension of the moment she shivered as it occurred to her how handsome he looked.

'You say you didn't think it your place to tell me? Not even after we'd been discussing it?'

Still she didn't reply, and he gave a sigh of exasperation. 'I just don't understand why, Frances.' He stood glaring at her with his hands on his hips, obviously waiting for some sort of explanation, and in the end she felt obliged to attempt to justify her silence.

'I didn't feel it was my place to tell you, Alex, because I was called out in a professional capacity and I felt it would be betraying a confidence.'

He frowned. 'I still don't understand. Just how much was Lucy involved?'

'I don't think to any great extent.'

'Then why couldn't you tell me? Did she ask you not to tell me?'

Frances shook her head. 'Not exactly, but she assumed that I would, so I felt compelled to tell her that I would respect her confidence.'

'When was that—at the beach?'

'No, the following morning,' she replied miserably.

'What happened the following morning?' he demanded. 'Where did you see her?'

'I was called out by Lucy to attend her friend Emma,' she said, then fell silent.

'And that's all you're going to tell me?'

She swallowed, for she could see that he was still very angry, then she nodded.

'For God's sake, Frances, I admire your ethics, but I am your trainer, and this is my daughter we're talking about!'

'In that case, Alex, I'm sorry but I think it would be better if you asked her yourself.'

'I thought it might be better if I heard the story from you first.' Without another glance he swung from the room, leaving Frances staring miserably at the tightly closed door.

She didn't know how she got through the rest of the afternoon, but somehow she coped with the remainder of the antenatal clinic. It was with a sigh of relief that she received the news from Lynne on the intercom that she had seen the last patient. Wondering if Alex was around, she made her way slowly out to Reception, then stopped as she saw a familiar figure at the desk talking to Beverley.

'I'm sorry, Lucy,' Beverley was saying, 'but your father's been called out to a road traffic accident. There's no telling how long he'll be.'

'Oh, I wanted to speak to him.' She stood uncertainly chewing the side of her thumb, and on a sudden impulse Frances hurried forward.

'Hello, Lucy,' she said as brightly as she could.

The girl turned sharply, and when she saw Frances she scowled.

'How about a cup of tea?'

'No, thanks, I came to try and make peace with Dad. We had the most frightful row earlier on,' she said, giving Frances an accusing stare. 'But apparently he's not here?'

'Well, how about a chat with me instead?'

Lucy glared at her for a moment as if carefully weighing her words, then, tossing back her long hair, she said bitterly, 'Don't you think you've done enough damage?'

Frances frowned, then realised that Lucy believed it was she who had told her father about the beach party. 'I think we need to talk, Lucy,' she said quietly. 'There are a few things we need to get straight.'

'I don't think I have anything to say to you,' replied Lucy, moving towards the door as she spoke.

'Lucy,' Frances made one last attempt, 'I'm your friend, you know; why don't you let me help?'

'If you call yourself a friend I certainly don't need any enemies,' the girl replied tightly, and, not giving Frances any further chance to explain, she marched out of the surgery.

As Frances turned she found Bea standing in the doorway of her consulting-room having obviously heard the whole thing. She raised her eyebrows at Frances, who shrugged helplessly.

The older woman frowned, then said quickly, 'Do you still fancy that cup of tea?'

'I can't think of anything better at the moment,' Frances replied wearily.

For once the staff-room was empty, and as Bea brewed the tea Frances sank down into an armchair, glad of a moment's respite to get her thoughts into order. From what Lucy had just said it was perfectly obvious that she had been placed squarely in the centre of the argument between Alex and his daughter. He blamed her for not telling him about his daughter's misdemeanours, and Lucy blamed her because she thought it had been Frances who had told him.

She sighed, then gratefully took the cup of tea that Bea handed to her.

'Problems?' Bea settled herself in the chair opposite Frances, helped herself to sugar and began to vigorously stir her tea.

Frances nodded, wondering how much she should tell Bea.

'Come on, spill the beans! It always helps, you know.'

Still she hesitated, then Bea sipped her tea and, placing the cup and saucer firmly on the coffee-table, crossed her arms and leaned back in her chair. 'It's you and Alex, isn't it?'

Frances looked startled. First Simon and now Bea—had they really made it that obvious?

Bea smiled when she saw her expression. 'Surely you didn't think you could keep it quiet in this place? Why, the mere fact that Sandra Jones is going around with a face like a thundercloud has been enough to arouse people's suspicions!'

Frances shrugged helplessly, but before she had the chance to say anything Bea rattled on, 'So, you're in love with our Dr Ryan?' Frances felt the colour flood her cheeks at the bluntness of the question, while Bea, having all the answer she needed, went on, 'And is he in love with you?'

'Yes, I think so,' Frances whispered.

'Then that's all that matters—end of story.' Bea gave her short bark.

'Not quite,' said Frances with a sigh. 'There are so many problems.'

'You don't mean that young lady down there in Reception?' Bea asked sharply, and when Frances nodded she said, 'What she needs is a smacked bottom—although I doubt that Alex would agree with me. He's made a few too many allowances for that young madam just because she lost her mother. So what's the problem? Jealousy?'

'I dare say that could ultimately be the problem,' said Frances drily, 'but it's not the immediate one. No, I'm afraid Miss Lucy Ryan thinks me guilty of a breach of confidence.'

Bea frowned, becoming serious as she stared at Frances. 'I think you'd better explain,' she said quietly.

Frances took a deep breath, then briefly, without going into too many details, she told Bea what had happened. When she had finished, Bea said, 'There isn't a problem, you know, Frances, and when you've had time to think about it you will realise that. You didn't betray that girl's confidence. God knows how Alex found out, but it certainly wasn't from you. You must now make sure that Lucy understands that.'

'But what about Alex?' said Frances miserably. 'He thinks it was my duty to tell him about his daughter.'

'Nonsense!' replied Bea with a snort, then standing up she looked down at Frances. 'He may have said that in the heat of the moment, but when he's had time to think about it, he'll think differently, you mark my words. Alex is your trainer, Frances, he'll admire what you did, you'll see.'

'I hope you're right,' replied Frances, still unconvinced. She glanced up when Bea remained silent and found her staring down at her with a strange expression on her face. 'What is it?' she asked curiously.

'I was just thinking. . .you said there were problems between you and Alex. What else is there?'

Frances sighed and replaced her cup and saucer on the table. 'He's worried about the age difference.'

'What is it? About twelve years?'

'Thirteen, to be exact.'

'That's nothing!'

'He's also concerned about the fact that he's my trainer. . .'

'Ah, I thought it might be something like that. . .but I can't see that it will matter—besides, he's only your trainer for a year, not for the rest of your lives!'

'You make it all sound so simple, Bea.'

'You have to, Frances—believe me, you have to. Don't go through life looking for problems, because if you do, you'll find them. If happiness comes, grab it by the throat and never let it go. Do you hear me?'

Her voice had become gruff, and as Frances stared at her in surprise at her sudden outburst, she found herself wondering if the rumours about her and Neville Chandler had been true and if Bea now wished she'd grabbed at happiness when she'd had the chance. She wasn't given the opportunity to ask, however, for Bea walked to the door, where she paused briefly and looked back.

'If I were you,' she said in the same gruff voice, 'I'd get over to Harbour Reach this minute and put things right.'

* * *

By the time that Frances was able to get away from the surgery it was evening, the sun was sinking behind the distant hills and the shadows were lengthening. She decided to walk to the harbour across the beach, and as she left through the gate in the walled garden she paused for a moment and looked across the sea. It was calm and tranquil, and Frances found it hard to believe that only forty-eight hours before it had been the raging monster that had claimed the life of one young man and very nearly that of a second.

As she approached the harbour steps and looked up at Harbour Reach drowsing gently in the rose-coloured glow from the setting sun, she felt her apprehension mounting. Had she been right to come, or should she have waited until Alex had sorted out his family problems and come to her?

Cautiously she climbed the steps, taking care not to slip on the green slimy lichen that clung to the stonework, then as she reached the top she saw that Alex's car wasn't in its usual place in front of the house.

She hesitated, then decided that maybe it was just as well that he wasn't at home so that she could have a chance to put things right with Lucy.

She rang the bell, then jumped as the door was immediately flung open and Jeannie Cameron stood on the threshold with her hands on her hips.

'Well, now, there's a coincidence!' she exclaimed, giving Frances no time to speak. 'We were just talking about you!'

'You were?' said Frances faintly as Lucy suddenly appeared behind Jeannie.

'Aye.' The woman stepped aside. 'You'd better come in. Lucy has something to say to you. She was about to pay you a visit, but you've saved her the trouble.'

Frances walked into the beautiful room and Jeannie shut the door behind her. To her surprise Frances saw that the girl looked embarrassed.

There was silence for a moment, then Jeannie said, 'Well, Lucy, go on.'

Lucy took a deep breath. 'I'm. . . I'm very sorry, Frances, for being rude to you earlier. I thought it was you who had told Dad about my being at the party; now I know it wasn't.'

'I see,' said Frances quietly, then, when it seemed that Lucy wasn't going to say any more, she asked, 'And do you know who it was?'

'Aye.' It was Jeannie who replied, and Frances turned to her questioningly. 'It was me.'

'You?' Frances's eyes widened in surprise. 'But how did you know?'

'There isn't a lot that goes on in this town that I don't know about. The lad whose life you saved, Frances, is the nephew of one of the ladies I play bridge with. She felt it her duty to inform me that Dr Ryan's daughter was one of the young people involved.' She paused and looked at Lucy, who was kicking at the edge of a rug with the toe of her shoe. 'Normally I wouldn't have told her father—heavens above, there've been enough occasions when I've covered up for her. . .' She paused.

'But this time. . .' prompted Frances.

'This time it was serious. . .really serious. A lad died. . .there was talk of drugs. . .and I felt Alex should be the one to handle it.'

'And has he handled it?' Frances looked at Lucy.

'Yes,' she mumbled. 'He's grounded me for two weeks. Two whole weeks! I wish I was dead.'

'You don't mean that, Lucy,' said Frances quietly, and Lucy had the grace to look shamefaced at her thoughtless remark.

'Well, no,' she said, 'perhaps I don't. But two weeks! In the holidays as well. . .' She turned away and walked across to the staircase, dragging her feet as she went. Mistoffelees was sitting on one of the steps and he arched his back, purring affectionately as she approached. She paused to stroke him then, looking back at Frances, she said, 'I didn't mean what I said about not needing any enemies,' she said.

'It's all right, Lucy,' said Frances. 'I know you didn't.'

The two women watched as she disappeared up the stairs, then as they heard her close her bedroom door Jeannie sighed. 'I don't envy you your task with that one,' she said.

'What do you mean?' Frances looked at her in surprise, but Jeannie carried on talking as if Frances hadn't spoken.

'Mind you, I've always said all she needed was a mother. She's a very talented girl. Alex must be made to understand, and if anyone can do it, you can.'

'I don't know what you mean. . .' began Frances, wondering just how many other people had guessed their so-called secret.

'Rubbish, of course you know,' said Jeannie, peering at her short-sightedly, then her tone softened. 'Mind you, I can't say I'm not delighted. I've done my best for those children because I felt I owed it to their mother, but the time has come now when I would like to move on and make something of what years I have left. I like you, Frances,' she stated bluntly. 'I won't worry leaving the children in your hands. Only the other day Nick told me how much he liked you, and you're right for Alex.'

Frances sighed. 'I wish someone would tell him that. He doesn't think I could cope with all the problems, and we seem to argue about everything under the sun. The latest argument was over Lucy— he thinks I should have told him about her being at the party.'

'Well, I think you might find he's changed his mind over that issue,' replied Jeannie firmly, then, as they heard the sound of a car outside, she added, 'But why don't you ask him for yourself?'

By the time Alex entered the front door Jeannie had disappeared upstairs and Frances was waiting for him alone.

He took one look at her, then gathered her into his arms, and for the second time in the space of an hour she found herself receiving an apology from a Ryan, and when she laughingly commented on just that, he grimaced. 'I wouldn't blame you if you weren't heartily sick of the whole bunch of us,' he said, then added, 'You were of course quite right about not betraying Lucy's confidence, and I should never have expected you to do so.' He frowned. 'But I'm glad that Jeannie told me. It could have got so much worse if I hadn't been aware of what was going on, but now that I know I can deal with it.'

'Don't be too hard on her, Alex,' said Frances softly. 'What she needs is lots of love along with firm handling—oh, and a little understanding, of course.'

'I suppose you mean over this drama school business,' Alex grunted. 'Well, maybe I have been a bit hard on her. Perhaps we could talk about it and work out some sort of compromise.' He pulled Frances closer to him, so failing to notice her secret little smile of happiness at his words.

Frances stayed for dinner with the Ryans and was delighted to find Nick and Jeannie accepting her like one of the family, and even Lucy seemed to have mellowed towards her, asking endless questions about her cousin James and his life in the theatre.

Later, when she said she should be getting back to the surgery, no one seemed surprised when Alex offered to walk her home.

They walked in silence for a while, then stood very close together, leaning against the rail and staring out over the quiet harbour with the many yachts at anchor, their sails lowered and their masts bare.

'I hope you'll never tire of this scene,' said Alex suddenly.

'Why?' She half turned her head so that she could look at his profile.

'Because I don't think I could bear to move away from here,' he replied.

She smiled. 'Am I to take that as a proposal, Dr Ryan?' she asked softly.

'I hope so, just as I hope you'll give me the answer I want.' He turned his head so that he could look into her eyes.

'And if I don't?' she teased.

'Then I shall have to exert my authority as your trainer and insist,' he replied with mock severity.

'Well, with that sort of threat hanging over me I have no choice but to accept,' she replied, adding curiously, 'But what about all those problems that were making it impossible for us to be together?'

'What problems? Are there any?' he asked innocently, then smiled and said, 'I'm sure there isn't anything that can't be sorted out, and if there is, then it can't be helped because I can't bear to be without you a moment longer.' Giving her no further chance to protest, he put his arms round her and his mouth found hers in a kiss that told her that all her fears had been for nothing.

Three women, three loves . . . Haunted by one dark, forbidden secret.

4 MEDICAL ROMANCES
AND 2 FREE GIFTS
From Mills & Boon

Capture all the excitement, intrigue and emotion of the busy medical world by accepting four FREE Medical Romances, plus a FREE cuddly teddy and special mystery gift. Then if you choose, go on to enjoy 4 more exciting Medical Romances every month! Send the coupon below at once to:

**MILLS & BOON READER SERVICE, FREEPOST
PO BOX 236, CROYDON, SURREY CR9 9EL.**

No stamp required

- - - ✂ - ✂ - - -

YES! Please rush me my 4 Free Medical Romances and 2 Free Gifts! Please also reserve me a Reader Service Subscription. If I decide to subscribe, I can look forward to receiving 4 Medical Romances every month for just £5.80 delivered direct to my door. Post and packing is free, and there's a free Mills & Boon Newsletter. If I choose not to subscribe I shall write to you within 10 days – I can keep the books and gifts whatever I decide. I can cancel or suspend my subscription at any time. I am over 18.

EP02D

Name (Mr/Mrs/Ms) ————————————————————

Address ————————————————————————

————————————————————————————

———————————————————— Postcode ————————

Signature ————————————————————————

-MEDICAL ROMANCE-

The books for your enjoyment this month are:

CARIBBEAN TEMPTATION Jenny Ashe
A PRACTICAL MARRIAGE Lilian Darcy
AN UNEXPECTED AFFAIR Laura MacDonald
SURGEON'S DAUGHTER Drusilla Douglas

Treats in store!

Watch next month for the following absorbing stories:

HEART SEARCHING Sara Burton
DOCTOR TRANSFORMED Marion Lennox
LOVING CARE Margaret Barker
LOVE YOUR NEIGHBOUR Clare Lavenham

Available from Boots, Martins, John Menzies, W.H. Smith, Woolworths and other paperback stockists.

Also available from Mills and Boon Reader Service, P.O. Box 236, Thornton Road, Croydon, Surrey CR9 3RU.

Readers in South Africa — write to:
Independent Book Services Pty, Postbag X3010, Randburg, 2125, S. Africa.